Sync

Chichima Cherry

Sync

A Novella

Chichima Cherry

Write and Vibe Publishing
Indianapolis

Published 2023

Printed in the United States of America

ISBN: 978-1-953430-19-9 (ebook)

978-1-953430-22-9 (pbk)

For information and permission requests, address:

Write and Vibe Publishing

P.O. Box 7004

Fishers, IN 46038

info@writeandvibe.com

Also By The Author

<u>Adult Reads (the spice is nice)</u>

Just Like Old Times - Dalton Family Book 1

Sync

Next Time Around - Dalton Family Book 2

Grown Girl Peace - Grown Girl Books (2027)

A Matter of Time - Dalton Family Book 3 (2027)

<u>Children's Books (each one teach one)</u>

Curiously Cara Meets Pharaoh Hatshepsut

Curiously Cara Meets Queen Amanirenas

<u>Inspirational/Spiritual Reads</u>

The Clouds Will Catch Me

A Note From Chi Chi

Hey Readers!

When I started *Sync* I had no idea where the story would go. Each week, I sat down and just let my imagination go. I had so much fun and also got to play around with drama and push my own boundaries.

As you'll see, Sync is connected to *Just Like Old Times*, the first novel in The Dalton Family series, so make sure to read that next to see how the stories intertwine. Sync will get her own romance novel but I write kinda slow so, sorry in advance for said delay. Additionally, you'll notice that I never completely physically described Sync. I did that because I felt like all of us could see a little of ourselves in her character.

I originally wrote this for Kindle Vella (no longer exists) so it is in more of an episodic format vs how I typically tell stories.

Regardless, this story still contains adult situations like explicit language and graphic sexual scenes, so it may not be suitable for younger audiences or sensitive readers.

Lastly, this story contains trigger warnings of on-the-page suicide attempt, death of family, adultery, and cheating. If those aren't your jam, I understand, more than you know.

As always, I wish you peace, prosperity, and joy.

~Chi Chi

Playlists

Listen to the Sync Playlist once, all the time, while reading, or during a long drive. Enjoy!

Scan Below for the Apple Music Playlist

Scan Below for the Spotify Playlist

Chapter 1

New Year, New Me

"TEN!"

Holding up my glass of champagne that, to be honest, was disgusting, I watched the New Year's Eve Ball work its way down that magical pole better than a stripper. With a drunken smile and ankles that barely held up after only an hour at a party that I wasn't invited to, I was sure that a tear would drop by the time we all yelled one.

To celebrate life, my girl, Nisha, and I had finagled our way into a VIP only party on the rooftop at a hotel club known best for the single to it's complicated but still successful and sexy men. I had yet to see one of those men but the night was young.

"NINE!" Men with opened suit jackets and loosened ties pumped their fists in the air.

"EIGHT!" Women in bralettes with bare midriffs screeched.

"SEVEN!" Drunkards yelled over the rooftop balcony overlooking a rowdy downtown.

"SIX!" Tears dropped from the inner corners of my eyes. Damn, we hadn't even reached one. If I didn't get it together I'd be a babbling mess and have to skirt off to the bathroom before

I got to kiss a stranger for good luck. I quickly dotted away my tears with my fingertips, careful not to smudge my makeup.

After recovering from one of the most emotional years of my life, this was my rebound year. Everyone loves to say things like this is my year and make breakable resolutions, but this really was my year. I felt it in my bones. To the core. Straight down to the blood that gave me happy fucking chills.

I'd spent most of last year getting to know myself and this year I was trying something different. I no longer wanted everything and anything. The only thing I craved was continued inner peace, joy, and freedom.

"ONE!" I screamed at the top of my lungs with the rest of the partygoers.

"Happy New Year, Sync!" Standing beside me, Nisha, wrapped her arm around my shoulders and planted a lipstick-stained kiss on my cheek. "Love you, Girl."

"Happy New Year, Nish! Love you, too." I squeezed her closer to me, spilling a few drops of champagne in the process.

Nisha was my extravagant queen. Her clothing? Bold. One of the many pairs of eyeglasses that she'd left behind tonight? Bold ass hot pink with black and white stripes. All facets of her personality were bold. Just last week she had tried her hand at bungee jumping. The next adventure she wanted to conquer was skydiving. When I grew up, I wanted to be just like her, even though we were only a year apart.

She turned us so that we were facing, then grabbed the tops of my shoulders. A huge smile on her face, she wiggled our shoulders and shrieked. "You made it another year. Happy birthday!"

No small feat considering my past. I jumped up and down, my gold sequin freak 'em dress slipping higher up my thighs with each jump. To anyone listening, which, surprisingly, was everyone around me, I yelled, "It's my birthday!"

A woman with flushed cheeks, most likely courtesy of the

small glass in her hand with a lime on the rim, pointed at me. "Somebody get this girl another drink! It's her birthday. And it's our new year." She looked around, waiting for a response but none came, which made me giggle. "This is gonna be our best year..." she continued but didn't get to finish her sentence, as a woman with long dark hair pulled her in for a tongue-filled smooch.

What I wouldn't give to be kissed like that. To feel passion pass from my lover to me. To have someone's hands tickle my skin. I was finally ready. Not for a relationship, but for a, umm, romance? A dick me down? Hell, I was ready for something.

My one free arm looped around Nisha's waist and together, we sang the new year song that people only pretend to know the words to. I actually knew the words but I'd also made up my own since this song coincided with my personal new year.

I gave it my all as loud as my voice would carry.

"May all my past years be for naught, and my fu-ture be bright! May allll my past years be for naught, and my fu-ture be bright!"

Nisha's and my body moved in time with the crowd, finishing up the song. As I looked at all the people that had gathered with only one intention, to celebrate making it through another year that many others hadn't come out of, happy tears bubbled up again.

It was nothing short of a miracle that I was standing next to Nisha today. Two hundred and seventy-eight days ago I'd tried to end it all.

My marriage to an almost perfect man was over. My choosing. I'd quit my job. Also, my choosing. The freedom of my choices was great at first, but then, I spiraled. Instead of my ex trying to persuade me to stay, he granted my wish. He never even fought for me. Wondering why he didn't choose me warred in my head with me not even wanting him to choose me in the first place. The consistent back and forth viciously tried my patience.

To ease my loneliness, I attempted to find a job but couldn't find a suitable one. It's hard to find the perfect job when the thought of working gives you invisible hives. With nowhere to go during the day, and nothing to do at night, all I did was sit with my thoughts. The longer I sat, the darker they became.

One day the darker thoughts intruded. Told me that if I was alone, what was the point of being around? It quickly went downhill from there. I suddenly remembered how much I missed my parents and brother, who had died in a car crash while on their way to my house for a Memorial Day cookout. Typically, thoughts of them brought me pleasant memories but since misery loves company, I trudged back down the road where I blamed myself for their deaths. Weeks went on and my depressive thoughts continued toward darkness. Next thing I knew, I was silently wishing to be hit by a bus. Or wondering if death would be instantaneous if I drove down a cliff.

I longed for my family. To be with them. To hear their voices again. I'd had enough of life without them. Life alone. I took some pills, grabbed my keys, and drove into a pole. I was launched out the window and unconscious before my car was practically split in two. Miraculously, I survived with only a few broken bones and recovered without permanent physical damage. I was still working on my mental but for what I'd been through I considered myself lucky.

Nisha squeezed my bicep and wiped my tears. "Are you okay?"

A small smile broke out on my face. I nodded, "Yes."

"Are you sure?" Worry splayed on her face as her eyes darted around mine, searching for signs of discontent. After my accident she'd sat with me every day at the hospital, made sure I never missed a therapy appointment, and that I took my antidepressants. She was the friend that everyone down on their luck needed in their life.

"Positive." I nodded again. "I'm happy, Nisha."

"Really?" her voice cracked.

"Yeah, Girl."

"I'm so relieved and happy to hear you say that."

"Me too. Now let's party!" Despite the taste, I downed the rest of my bubbly in one gulp and then threw the glass over everyone's heads and into the brick wall across the room. The roof went quiet but then erupted into cheers and laughter. Those who saw me pitch my glass celebrated by pumping their fists in the air and smacking my ass. I ate it all up.

Nisha held her stomach, nausea playing with her mind. "I can't believe you just did that," she yelled over the music that had started back up.

I shrugged, "Me neither."

"New year, new you!"

"Hell yeah." We screamed obscenities into the air.

"I should do it too!" Nisha wobbled into me, her hand landing on my shoulder to stabilize herself. "New year, new me!"

"Do it, Nish!"

She pulled the hem of her dress down and drew back her arm, ready to do her own version of glass smashing. Before she could do so, her ankle gave way and she slipped on the floor, taking me with her. As I lay on top of her, chest to chest, most likely with my ass and hers hanging out of our dresses, I couldn't stop laughing.

Strong arms wrapped around my waist and lifted me back onto my feet. Another man lifted up Nisha. We turned around to finally see one of those sexy men. Next to him was another one. Whether caused by the liquor or the abundance of male pheromones seeping through his skin, I flung myself into the arms of the man that had lifted me up.

His deep brown eyes looked into mine and he smiled. "It's time for you to leave."

"Back to your place or mine?" I heard myself whisper.

He laughed, louder than necessary and that's when I saw the badge on his shirt that read, Security. "Definitely not mine, I'm married. And happily." He removed my hands from his shoulders. "You can't go around throwing glasses at walls so you gotta go. I'll escort you and your friend out. There are cars downstairs and they'll take you wherever you need to go."

I looked behind me and saw Nisha being carried out by the other security guard like a princess. One hand was caressing the man's bald head and the other was stroking his beard. He set her down on the sidewalk next to me and signaled for a car.

Before closing the car door, the security guard that walked me out leaned into the car. "Happy birthday." He winked and officially shut the door on our night.

The woman in the driver's seat turned around. "Three rules. Don't throw up in my car. Don't piss or shit in my car. Don't trash my car. Breaking any of those rules will get you dropped off at the police station where your drunk asses will be forced to sober up. Now, where am I taking you?"

Nisha had already fallen asleep so I gave the address and leaned back. This was the best New Year's Eve I'd had in over fifteen years.

Chapter 2

I Met a Guy

THE TEXT GLARED AT ME JUST AS HARD AS I GLARED BACK AT MY phone. I hated Nisha for remembering today's date and loved her even more for checking on me. Today was the anniversary of the day my ex-husband boarded a plane for paradise and left me behind. The day I'd driven him to the airport, hugged him goodbye, passionately kissed him one last time, and adamantly assured him that, yes, I was still choosing to end our marriage. It was the day my world split into a before and an after.

When I went to respond, a deep sigh escaped but the tears stayed inside. Even though I didn't regret my decision, there were times when I second guessed it. It's not like I ended our marriage because he cheated or disrespected me. It wasn't even because I had stopped loving him. The problem came about because at some point I stopped loving myself, and that wasn't okay. Therefore, I had to leave.

Library?

Yep

The library was my place of solace. Whenever I wanted to break free from my thoughts, I always ended up there. There was something about knowing that whatever I picked up, I'd be reminded that happily ever after did, in fact, happen, werewolves existed, and some people's lives were worse than mine.

Nisha returned my text with a sad face smiley and told me she'd be over in an hour for dinner and mimosas. A tradition we resorted to whenever one of us were emotionally under the weather.

Thx. See u later

I stashed my phone back in my purse and ignored the emptiness building in the pit of my stomach. Deep breaths. I needed deep breaths. I lifted my wrist and tapped the button on my smart watch that guided me through a breathing series. I desperately needed to quell the tiny voice that kept whispering, You chose wrong.

On my final breath, I opened my eyes and focused on the books on the shelves in front of me. Even if my stomach was still quaking, my mind was a smidge clearer. Slowly walking along the carpeted floor, I ran my fingers along the spines, waiting for a book to catch my attention.

When a cookbook with one hundred and fifty ways to change my eating habits for the new year called out to me, I paused. I wasn't a chef, nor did I intrinsically love cooking, but quite possibly, there was something in there that I needed to see. Opening it up, the bright pictures of the dishes called out to me. Yes, this one was coming home.

"Excuse me," came a voice from behind me, causing me to drop the cookbook on the ground.

"Shit!" I harshly whispered. My hand flew to my chest and I turned around only to come face to face with a man wearing dark sunglasses, a neatly trimmed beard, a black puffer coat, and a grey skull cap pulled low on his forehead. The untied boots on his feet added a nice, rugged touch.

He picked up the cookbook and handed it to me. "I'm sorry. I didn't mean to startle you."

"No, it's fine." I continued to come down from my adrenaline rush. "I just didn't hear you walk up."

"Sorry about that."

"Really, it's fine. Was I in your way?" I stepped away from the spot I'd been standing in to make way.

"Actually, no, you weren't in my way. I was here a couple weeks ago and I saw you here, or at least I think it was you. I told myself that if I saw you again, I'd introduce myself. To say hello."

My expression froze as I tried processing the last time I'd been here and whether I'd seen him. As handsome as he appeared to be I think I would've noticed him. Wouldn't I have?

"I was getting out my car and you were walking down the stairs, so you probably didn't see me. I just figured it was you, not many people have the same red coat."

I looked down and nodded with a smile on my face. "Yeah, they probably don't; it is pretty bright. And I was here two weeks ago so most likely, it was me."

A relieved expression flitted across his features. "Cool. I'm Isaiah."

"Sync." I held out my hand, which he gently took, allowing his thumb to briefly caress the inside of my palm.

"Pleasure to meet you, Sync. You're even more beautiful up close."

"Thank you."

"You're welcome." Isaiah released my hand. "I like your name. Very unique."

"Yeah."

"So, a cookbook. What are you planning on making?"

I glanced at the book in my hand. "Nothing in particular. I'm just going through a phase and wanted to check out some recipes."

"Gotcha. I always find it inspiring when people can just throw shit together and not only does it look good, but it tastes good, too. I'm never that lucky."

His sense of humor made it easy to laugh along with him. "It's an art, that's for sure. So, what are you checking out today?"

A slight smirk lifted the corner of his mouth and although I couldn't see his eyes under his sunglasses, my intuition told me that the silence before his response meant that he'd turned my question into an inuendo. This man was turning my day around.

"I was trying to find *Devil in a Blue Dress*. The librarian sent me this way and as luck would have it, I ran into you first. Do you happen to know where it is?"

He stepped closer and I took a deep inhale of his cologne. Colognes were a guilty pleasure of mine. When I wasn't in a library, I enjoyed scent browsing and could now recognize most of them. Isaiah's was spicy with a hint of sweetness and cedarwood. Sweet Baby Jesus, he was wearing my all-time favorite cologne, Burberry Hero.

I quietly moaned as I took another inhale. When his eyebrow shot up, I quickly played it off. "Uhm hmm, yes, I know where it is. I'll show you. It's actually just across the aisle." I pointed to the other section. His gaze followed mine and then he turned back to me.

We fell into step for the brief walk to the other bookshelves and when we stopped, I gave him another onceover. He wasn't huge in stature, maybe five-foot-ten or eleven, but he presented a larger than life feel. Not particularly bulky, not particularly small, but underneath his outerwear I could tell his body was well maintained. And he was in a library, hopefully that meant he was also intelligent.

I perused the shelves looking for *Devil in a Blue Dress*. "It should be here somewhere." To see the titles at my waist level, I bent over and rested my hands on my knees but then swallowed hard, wondering if he had taken the opportunity to look at my ass. I bit the corner of my lip and swiveled around to see that yes, he had, and he wasn't trying to hide it. I found the book and then stood. It had been so long since a man had shown interest in me that I felt completely out of my element. My cheeks instantly flushed.

"Here you go."

A slow smile spread across his ebony tinted skin and he juggled the book in his fingertips. He waited a beat before asking, "What are you doing after you leave here? I was gonna get some ice cream. Would you like to join me?"

I looked to the window behind him, to the snowflakes falling to the ground like we were inside of a snow globe. "Ice cream in the winter?"

"Does one not eat ice cream when it's cold?" Isaiah challenged.

"One does, it's just not something you hear people say they're going to do very often in January."

"You only live once," he raised his eyebrows.

"Take off your sunglasses for me."

"Excuse me?"

"Take off your sunglasses, please. I'd like to see your eyes so I know I haven't been talking with a psychopath this entire time."

He chuckled, a low rumble that flitted across my skin. "You can tell all of that from looking into my eyes?"

"I can do all of that and more."

He slowly removed his sunglasses as if he was removing his clothes on a stage. Whether I blamed it on my sex drought or my emotional state of mind, my thoughts were all bad. His lashes were long, his eyes, set deep under his thick eyebrows. The stark brown color in the oval shape was thinly stretched across his face to where I almost questioned whether he could see through the slits. Seeing his full face with his square jawline and the perfectly lined hair almost made me want to go anywhere with this stranger, especially to his bed.

"This better?"

"It is, but..."

"There's a but. Looks like I'm eating ice cream alone."

"I don't wanna run off with a stranger."

"I'm not a stranger, I'm Isaiah. Isaiah Jones to be exact."

"Well, Isaiah Jones, I do already have plans for this evening."

He nodded and rested his shoulder on the bookshelf next to us, devoting all of his attention to me. "I understand. Maybe another time."

"I'd like that."

"I'd need your number for that." He handed me his phone and I saved my number in his contacts. With an intensity that I hadn't felt in years, he asked, "Can I walk you to your car, Sync?"

Once in my car I drove home with a smile that stayed on my face for the entire ride. Nisha was already waiting in my driveway when I got there. She exited her car with grocery bags in her hand and I grabbed what I could carry.

"Hey, girl, you don't look as sad as you seemed earlier. You feeling better?"

"I am." The large smile from my car ride home returned. "I met someone."

Chapter 3

Roller Baddie

"I HAVE JUST THE GUY," NISHA SAT ON THE SOFA NEXT TO ME with a goofy smile on her face. Mimosas and dinner were officially done and to keep it real, my mimosas had transferred into strictly champagne about three mimosas ago.

"Nisha, no," I waved her off. "I'm not having sex with a random guy. Plus, I just met someone."

"You don't even know Isaiah and it could be months before you two have sex. And might I mention, he hasn't even texted you yet."

"It's only been a few hours," I grumbled.

"If he hasn't hit you up yet then technically, it's like he doesn't even exist. Just pretend you haven't met Isaiah. And this guy isn't random; I know him."

I crossed one arm over my other. "I can't believe you're trying to put me out there for a sexual hookup."

"It's better than a dating app hookup, don't you think?" Nisha rubbed my biceps and looked me in the eye as if she had some life changing statement to make. "Sync, you start work at a new job on Monday and that's stressful enough. Add to that,

13

you've already been stressed because of regular life and you haven't had sex in forever. You need this."

"I don't need a casual fling. I'm a classy girl."

Nisha fell back on the sofa and burst out laughing. "I know you fuckin' lying!"

"Nisha!"

When she calmed down she said, "Think of this as more of a sexual revolution. A coming of sexual age. This is the beginning."

I remained quiet. A sexual revolution kind of sounded intriguing.

She continued, "You were never wild. Not before your divorce. Not after. It's time to let your hair down. Find out what you like and what you love, sexually. Trust, you need this. You never know, you could like being choked but how would you know if you never tried?"

"I can't believe I'm entertaining this."

Nisha flopped on the sofa, filled with giddiness. "So, you're entertaining it?" I just sighed. "Have I ever let you down?"

"Never, but there's always a first time for everything."

She gave me the finger. "Law is everything you need."

"Law? His name is Law? This keeps getting better. What else do you know?"

Nisha bit her lip as she tried to think of something else.

I sat up so fast that I almost spilled what was left of my mimosa. "You don't know anything else about him?"

"It's not like me and him talk, Sync. But going by the way he skates, I know he got that stroke and can show you a good time."

This was what my life had resorted to. My friend thinking that I was so prude and stressed that she needed to find me a fuck buddy on skates. I set down my glass and threw my arms out to the side in surrender. "Okay, why not?"

"Aye!" Nisha shuffled into the kitchen and brought me back

a second slice of strawberry cheesecake. "Eat while I find you an outfit. If my instincts are right, you'll need your energy."

I drained the contents of my glass and followed her back to my bedroom. She had already pulled a pair of black knee-high socks with white stripes, cotton booty shorts with the signature Adidas emblem, a jean shirt button up, and a tankini out of my drawers.

"Where did you pull those from that fast?"

She shrugged with the biggest smile on her face. "It's a talent."

"I never would've put those clothes together."

"Also, a talent." She shoved the clothes into my hands. "Now go get dressed."

From inside my bathroom, I yelled to her. "I only have one rule for tonight. If I'm not feeling Law, then I'm out of there."

"Obviously."

Sitting on the bench, I was having serious second thoughts, so I took my good ol' time lacing up my skates. "I can't believe I let you talk me into this."

"Let's be honest, it didn't take much. Anyway, you'll thank me when Law is doing exactly what Smokey said he'd do to Mrs. Parker."

I tried to disguise my laugh as I elbowed her in her side. "You make it seem like abstinence is a bad thing."

"It is."

"It isn't. I was..."

"I know, I know, you were working on you."

"Exactly."

"Well, it's time for someone else to work on you." She smiled and pulled my hand toward the rink. "Let's go." Right before we entered, she rolled the bottom of my shorts to right up under my crotch and then pulled the pockets down so that they showed at the bottom. The last thing she did was take the bottom of my shirt and tie it in a knot at my belly button. She smiled and bobbed her head like she was in a music video. "She ready."

"I was already ready before you made me look like you. I look good on my own, I don't need all this."

"Listen," she sidestepped a group of women coming in from the rink with tees that read Roller Baddies. They were dressed just like us. "On a normal day, you don't need this. But here, tonight, this is what will bring all the attention to you and honey, you are the baddest out here. I'm gonna go find Law."

"Nisha," I called after her, but she'd already left me in her dust. It wasn't long before the thumping music swept me away and the announcer had the nerve to say, "Couples only. Couples only. Fellas, grab your woman and her ass. And if you ain't got a partner, get the hell out my rink."

Figures we'd arrive right as couples skate was starting. I was making my way out when a man skated over to me, approaching so fast that I got nervous he'd knock me over. He caught me and we spun around before stopping.

Hands around my hips, skate to skate, he licked his lips. "Sync?"

I nodded. "Law?"

He drew his bottom lip into his mouth and took my hand in his. Nisha was right about everything she'd managed to tell me about Law. There was just something about him that made you weak in the knees. He was taller and thinner than I preferred but his swag spoke for itself. The hair on his head couldn't have been more than a couple inches and it wildly ran in all directions.

Midway through the song he spun around and skated backwards so that he was facing me. Hands in his, he said, "I'm here all the time and you're not. You're either new to skating or new to town. Which is it?"

"I've lived here forever but I haven't been here in a long time. My girl dragged me down here tonight. Sort of a stress reliever after a bad day."

He looked at me and smiled, showing a couple platinum teeth, proving he had a rough edge. "Sorry you had a bad day, Sync." He pulled me closer and wrapped his arms around my waist, "Follow my lead so we don't fall. I don't plan on being horizontal with you until later."

As bold and forward as he was, I had to admit that I liked it and craved more. We had only made one lap around before Nisha hurriedly skated over. "Sorry to interrupt but I need to talk to you, now!"

Law released my waist and turned back around to skate next to me.

"Can't it wait," I asked through clenched teeth. Everything about tonight was Nisha's idea and now she was cock blocking.

"No."

"No worries, Shorty. I'll be waiting when you come back." He winked and skated away. Nisha had better have a good reason for the intrusion.

"What's so urgent?"

She yanked my hand and led me between a row of lockers. She peeked around them and pressured me to do the same. "*That's* what's urgent. Your ex is here!"

My mouth dropped open as I looked at the back of my ex-husband's body standing at the concession stand with another woman. He wasn't a skater, and he should've been living out of the country, but there was no question about whether that was him. I'd know that figure anywhere.

"What do you wanna do?" Nisha asked.

Chapter 4

Ex Factor

"Are we disappearing or staying?" Nisha asked when I still hadn't answered. As hard as I tried, I couldn't get my mouth to cooperate with my brain. Even if I could, cottonmouth kept me from uttering one word.

The man I had abandoned stood in line, most likely planning to order a nacho with cheese and a hot dog. I knew this because those were his guilty pleasures. Every time he attended the fair or a sports game, he always ordered double nachos and one beef hot dog.

Every memory of us, of him, rushed forward, emotionally knocking me off balance.

Why was he back in the states? Was it an emergency? Was he here temporarily or was he permanently home? Would he have let me know he was back? We'd sold our house so where was he staying? I had so many questions.

Nisha gently pulled on my arm. "Let's get out of here."

In all the time we'd been separated, and now divorced, I hadn't once thought about what I'd say or how I'd react if I ever saw him again. If I had, maybe I would've been more prepared.

In a tone that I barely recognized, I whispered, "Okay."

Just as we were preparing to dart back out of sight, I saw the woman next to him place her hand on his chest. He returned the gesture by pulling her closer. They were together?

My whole body went numb. I assumed this was what a heart attack felt like. While I hadn't expected him to pine over me and wallow in his feelings – and clearly, I'd been the cause of our relationship's demise, but shit, this hurt more than anticipated.

As if he felt me, as if our bond had never been severed, he looked my way. I watched as his face changed from surprise, to panic when he removed his arm from the woman, to anger when he balled his hands into fists, to intrigue when his eyes casted a dance over my figure, and finally to interest, as he told the woman he'd be right back and left her standing in line alone.

"I think it's too late to leave," my brain finally connected to my mouth.

"It's never too late for anything," Nisha reminded me.

"I've hurt him enough. I deserve whatever he has to say to me. I can't leave now."

"Want me to stay with you or watch from the sidelines?"

"Sidelines." I put on my big girl panties and waited for him to approach.

Nisha squeezed my hand in support before skating away. She waved at Kenneth on her way to the rink, to which he waved back. That, at least, was a sign that pointed toward him not hating her, nor me.

Waiting for him to reach me was a special kind of torture. My brain whispered that I could never truly fall out of love with the person that had loved me so well. My nerves reminded me that whatever words he decided to release on me – I wasn't prepared.

"Hey, Amber." He stopped so close in front of me that

others might have thought we were together. "I didn't expect to see you here."

We both laughed awkwardly. And then laughed again because even after a year, we were still on the same wavelength.

"I didn't expect to see you here either. Are you back from Nassau?" I asked.

"I am, permanently. The firm I was working with decided not to renew the contract. I thought for sure they would but I'm terrible at predicting things."

"I'm sorry to hear that." And I was. "That's surprising."

"You're telling me."

"Well, even though it ended, why didn't you stay? Get another contract or job there? It seems like such a beautiful place to live. That's what I would've done."

"You didn't even come so how do you know you would've stayed?"

Was that a jab? I looked down, allowing my eyes to wander the place before looking back at him. Surprisingly, he wasn't holding a grimace. He was actually smiling. "What's funny?"

"You are, I guess. You've changed a little physically but you're still the same person. I like your hair by the way."

"Thanks," I ran my fingers through it. After I'd healed from my accident, I went from long, naturally curly hair to practically a taper. It was so short that I had the barber cut an infinity sign into it right above my temple. As much as the infinity sign symbolized a way to remember that life was always worth continuing on, it was also symbolic of the blending of Amber's pain with my present and future. Learning how to be one with myself. Learning how to live in sync.

Because I was all for grand, symbolic gestures, I'd started going by Sync. Sync Amber Patterson.

I'd since let my hair grow out to a short, relaxed bob and I loved this length and how it fit me.

"Now, that outfit, that's not your norm but you look good in it." His voice lowered as he finished his sentence. I felt heat settle in between our bodies. I'd missed Ken. A lot. I'd missed so many things, including the way he handled my body in the bedroom. He'd explored every crevice on my body. Besides a pitiful one-night stand after our separation, I hadn't been with anyone else.

I chuckled and rubbed the back of my neck. "I don't normally dress like this. Somewhere in between what you see here and what you remember, is what I wear now."

"I always liked how you dressed but this is nice, too." He surveyed the rink and looked around. "Are you able to go somewhere so we can talk? Some place quieter?"

I knew my husband. EX! I knew my ex-husband and he didn't just want to talk. He'd seduce me and he was damn good at seduction.

I checked my phone. "It's almost eleven. And won't your friend be upset that you're ditching her?"

"My friend? Oh, my friend." He glanced back to the concession stand. The woman waved to me and I waved back. "Naw, she won't care. It's not like that."

Even though he brushed it off like it was nothing, the look on the woman's face after Ken turned his head said otherwise. "You don't need to protect my feelings. It's okay if you moved on, Ken."

"To be honest, she thinks it's more than it is, but I'd ditch her for you any day."

I crossed my arms across my chest and shook my head. "Don't say things like that. If someone did to me what I did to you I'd hate them."

"Hate is a strong word, and I could never feel that for you." He released a deep sigh. "Amber, we have a lot to talk about. If not tonight, then when?"

I didn't know. It was hard enough seeing him and realizing that regardless of how I ended things, feelings were still there.

Why couldn't it end where we'd left it? Apparently, I still needed to get over him.

"What's your new number?" he persisted. "You at least owe me an explanation of what happened to make you not want to be with me."

Entitlement reared its ugly head, but I couldn't say I wouldn't have said the same. "Do I?"

"Do you what?"

"Do I *owe* you an explanation? Yes, it would be nice to provide you with one but we're divorced, I don't owe you anything anymore."

"Damn, Amber." He took a step back and his eyes turned cold. "That's messed up. I loved you and provided for you and cared for you the way I was supposed to. You never said you were unhappy. You never said you were sad. Or lonely. Or anything. You blindsided me. Stuck a knife in my back and waved as I got on the plane. I took that job in The Bahamas because you said you always wanted to live on a beach. I did everything for you. So yes, you *do* owe me an explanation. That's the least you could do."

I couldn't help but shake my head. I wanted to outright skate away from his ass for thinking he could demand anything from me, but I did care about him and he was right. We would talk and then we'd both have the closure we needed. I read off my numbers as he typed them in his phone and sent me a text. "I'll call you tomorrow."

Ken was about to skate off when he stood straighter, almost as if on alert, his shoulders squared. I turned to see what had caught his attention and saw Law walking over. He'd taken off his skates and replaced them with a pair of Jordans.

He turned toward Ken, "Sorry to interrupt, Man. Excuse us for just one minute." He turned our backs to Ken and lowered his voice. "I was gonna leave but your homegirl said you might be tryna get into something tonight." He paused and licked his lips. "Is you?"

This was turning out to be a hell of a time. Law's eyes held the perfect promise of a great night and regardless of how I was feeling, he was what I needed. I took a chance on me, as I'd learned to do over this past year. I was getting my stress relief tonight. "Give me a minute and I'll be right over."

"Bet." He walked away and I turned around to face Ken.

"He's no good for you." Ken's lips stayed in a tight line while he watched Law move across the rink.

"I'll talk to you later, Ken. Have a good night."

"You do the same," he spoke through gritted teeth.

Chapter 5

Law

I WAS NERVOUS AS HELL SITTING NEXT TO LAW IN HIS OLD SCHOOL Monte Carlo. He hadn't made much conversation since we'd left the rink, but I needed him to say something. Anything to keep all my thoughts off Ken and his return to the states. I still couldn't believe he was back. For good. I wanted that to mean nothing but with him wanting to talk, I worried I would forget I wanted to remain single until I loved myself as much as, if not more, than I loved anyone else.

"You good over there?" Law's question broke into my thoughts.

"Yeah, I'm fine. Thanks." My hands shook a bit as I rubbed them down my thighs, wiping away the moisture that my nervous energy had created.

Law looked away from the night drive to glance at me. His eyes casted a glance at my hands first. "That dude you was talking to looked like he was stressing you out."

Stressing me out was an understatement. "Just a little bit. He's, umm, he's my ex-husband."

"Damn. I knew he was someone you used to be serious with by the way he was looking at me. If we was in another spot with less people he would've fought me for interrupting y'all little chat." He chuckled a bit.

I didn't respond. Ken had no right to harbor protective feelings over me but under the circumstances, I understood. The last time we'd seen each other we'd been married. Now...we weren't. I looked over to see Law lightly stroking the hairs in his short beard.

"Shorty, I'm a keep it one hundred. You and me, we don't know each other all like that. And I don't know what kind of niggas you usually go for but I'm guessing it ain't me-probably more like your ex. But since you left with me, I consider myself the luckiest mutha fucka that was at the rink tonight."

I thought of all the negativity that came with my past. All of the deaths that surrounded my life. My depression that crept back up whenever it felt like it. None of that made me lucky to be around. Sure, I looked good on the outside, but my inner was fucked up. "Get to know me better before you go thinking you're lucky."

"I saw everything I needed to see. Heard everything I needed to hear. My gut tells me I'm the lucky one and my gut ain't never led me down the wrong path," Law insisted.

We pulled into a gas station and he grabbed a wad of cash out of his pocket. He unrolled three twenties and stashed the rest. "I'm gon' make sure you have a good rest of the night. I ain't here to add no more stress. What you want to drink? You probably drink fancy wine like Pinot Noir or some shit."

An unexpected laugh bubbled up because it was true. I loved a good Pinot. He turned to me with a smile turned up at the corner of his mouth. That was sexy as hell, even with his platinum teeth. "See, I knew it. My gut always right. That's what you want? The Pinot?"

"I'll take that or anything else that's sweet."

"You talkin' 'bout Moscato?"

I nodded with a short smile. "Yeah, that's cool, too. Thank you."

He cupped the bottom of my chin. "I got you, for as long as you let me. Remember that. Lock the doors. Sometimes them meth heads be outta pocket. I'll be right back."

I could handle myself, or at least I liked to think so, but I counted the minutes until I saw Law's lean body reappear in the door frame. His thick gold and silver chains caught the light underneath his coat as he walked toward me. I knew nothing about this man. We'd probably spent a total of ten minutes together, max, and now I was headed to his place. Ken's words rang in my ear, "He's no good for you."

He wasn't, but I was ready to be a bit bad. To indulge in something that was no good for me. I was taking a hell of a chance tonight but like Law, my instincts told me it was safe enough. Still, I double checked to assure I was still sharing my location with Nisha. From there, it was on. My inhibitions were off and whatever Law gave tonight, I was receiving. The thought of what he'd do made me bite the corner of my bottom lip.

I. Couldn't. Wait. My hand brushed against his when he dropped in his seat and handed me the bag with my beverage inside. I swallowed before releasing a deep breath. "Thanks."

"You're welcome." He checked me out, noticing the lust that had appeared on my face. A wicked smile appeared before his gaze drifted to my parted lips. The air sizzled without a sound as I waited for his mouth to cover mine. He licked his lips and placed his hand on my exposed thigh. At first, his hand stroked my skin. Back and forth. Back and forth. Then, he gently squeezed the flesh, his rough hands a welcoming sensation against my soft skin. His touch was phenomenal.

"From this point, you only thinking of me." He leaned over the console, his eyes as low as his voice. "Come over here, Shorty."

His hand palmed the back of my head when I leaned

forward. Quite the opposite of what I expected, his touch continued to be gentle. Even, loving. His lips barely touched mine at first, but then he pushed further into me, sipping on my lips as if they were a fine cognac. His other hand, still on my thigh, squeezed in the same motion as our lips moved. The squeezing and stroking on my thigh combined with the sensual movements of our lips was exotic. On the last squeeze, I moaned into his mouth.

When we parted, all I could process was to lay my head against the headrest. I was officially in Law's world. This would be a night to remember.

His voice still low, he said, "I don't have a lot of physical shit but I know how to treat a woman and I'm gonna treat you right. That cool with you?"

"Yeah," I croaked out.

The rest of the ride was silent besides the slowed down music thumping through his amped up speakers. His hand continued to caress my thigh in all the right places. It had been so long since I'd been touched like that that I started to squirm in my seat, anxiously awaiting the arrival to his home. His fingers danced along my thigh, finding a tender spot I didn't know existed.

I couldn't wait to feel him between my thighs. Which would he choose to use first? His finger? His tongue? If I was as lucky as he thought he was, it would be the instrument now straining against his pants.

Thoughts of what awaited me once we made it to his bed had me instinctively massaging my breasts through my shirt. It'd been a long time, but I knew exactly where my body craved to be touched. His eyes watched my streetlight highlighted movements but he never said a word. By the time we pulled into his driveway I was close to the edge. One kiss and I would catapult into orgasm oblivion.

If you asked me where he lived, I couldn't tell you. Or how

we got there? I'd be clueless. All I know is that the moment he locked the door to his house behind us, his body pressed up against mine and pushed me into the wall, his needing dick pressing into the arch of my back. *This* already felt like everything I'd been awaiting.

His hand went to my throat, gently coaxing its way up to my neck. He tilted my chin to look into his eyes. Inch by inch, he brought his head toward mine. I was already on fire for his lips to touch mine again but instead, he brushed our cheeks together. My mouth parted on a sigh.

"I like that show you put on in my car. We gonna keep that up." He placed slow kisses from my ear, along my jawline, and back up to the soft spot under my ear. "Come on, let's play."

He took my hand, guiding me down the dark hallway to what I hoped was his bedroom. Before he opened the door he paused and turned toward me. Hands on my waist, he drew me closer. My feet bumped up against his. He bit his lip and just when I thought he'd kiss me, he said, "I hope you ready."

If the pool of liquid in my panties was any indication, I'd been ready for the past thirty minutes. I looked up at him through my lashes, my hands rubbing up and down his chest. "I am."

"Good." Law led me inside his bedroom and pushed me back up against the closed the door so that my back was to his chest again. He had to be an ass man. Still unable to see, all my senses were involved and on high alert. I was completely willing to let him do anything to me. Anywhere. His full lips gently touched my shoulder and then laid a kiss a little bit further over. And then a little bit higher until he closed in on my hairline.

"I like kissing you."

I liked it too but I was a fiend who needed more. I moaned as I pressed my breasts into the wall and my ass further into him. He pushed back into me, lighting a fire in my core.

"Shorty, you ain't got no control in here. You come when I let you."

So he knew I was close. Knew I needed more. I pressed into him harder. It had been almost a year since I'd had a man inside of me. Almost a year of wondering if I still knew how to be with a man. Too many days of asking myself if I was sexy enough to attract a man. I needed Law and hoped he would be my everything for the night. I needed his lips on mine. I needed his hands on my bare skin.

The thought of it had me trying to turn around. He stopped me from moving by tightening his grip on my hips. His voice growled into the back of my neck, right in between the crevices of my spine. "Everything you do in this room is gon' be what I told you to do. Now go stand in front of that bed."

I did as told. Truth is, I would've done anything Law told me to do. If he told me to use a plug, I would. If he commanded me to swallow, I would. He held the power over me and my body to make me do things I'd never consider.

"You was looking good as fuck in them skates down at the rink." He rose off the door he was leaning against and stalked closer to me. "I seen you soon as you walked in with your girl." He was almost in front of me and I could make out his features. Those full lips would be my demise. "Every dude in that jawn seen you walk in, but I knew you was goin' home with me."

He stopped so close that I could feel the heat from his body. "Take off your shirt."

I started to pull it off in a hurry, but his voice commanded, "Slowly."

I untied my top shirt, shrugged out of it, and let it drop from my fingertips to the ground.

"Now, that other shirt you got on. Pull that shit off."

I hesitated at first but then went for it. My breasts swung in my bra as I lifted my shirt over my head.

He growled. "You got nice ass titties." He bent down and

placed gentle kisses on the tops of my breasts. I didn't know if I could touch him, but I didn't care. My hands needed to feel him. To remind me that this was real. A hand on each side of his head, I lightly ran my thumbs along his ears.

He kissed my breasts a couple more times before he removed my hands, kissing the palms before letting them fall to my side. "Take off your shorts."

He took a step back to watch me in action. I unbuttoned the top button, then the next two.

"Shit," Law groaned out. His hand began massaging his dick through his pants. "Now that zipper, Shorty."

My hands glided my zipper downwards.

"Yeah, just like that. Don't take them off though." His voice sounded rough, as if he was calling on all his power to stay in control. Law dropped to his knees in front of me, running his hands from the backs of my knees, up my thighs to the bottoms of my shorts, and up higher to the curve of my ass, where he squeezed.

"Fuck," he rasped out. "You got a BBL or this all you?"

My hands running through his wild hair, I breathed out, "Mine."

"I like the sound of that. Just like you mine tonight." He continued to knead my skin, taking his time with the process like I wasn't craving more.

"Law, please."

He glided my shorts down my hips and then resumed his position with his nose against my panties. He inhaled deeply, taking in the scent of my arousal. His hands shook as they went back to running up and down my skin. "Tell me what you want me to do."

Chapter 6

A Night with Law

Law kissed the skin above my panty line and then traced an invisible line with his tongue up to my belly button, causing me to release his name on a gasp. "Tell me, Shorty, what you want?"

What did I want? I wanted him. Every part of him. His body grinding on top of me, thrusting from underneath me, and moving inside of me, but he had me so breathless that I couldn't express a damn thing.

Law rose to his full height, wrapped his arms around my neck to pull me even closer, our bodies bumping into each other, and he backed me up against the bed. His tongue moistened his lips before he brought his head down to mine. His breath on me, his eyes lowered, he yanked me into him.

"You like it rough?" He kissed me hard, smashing our lips together before pulling away. "Or you like that romantic, love making type shit?" He came back down and his lips took over mine. They were so soft against mine. He took his time guiding me, getting to know the curves of my mouth.

When he finally pulled away, I grabbed for him, not

wanting our connection to end. "Both ways feel good. I think I like it both ways."

He smirked, taking a step back, and I watched, waited for his next move. He wasted no time throwing his coat on the chair in the corner of the room. Then he pulled off his shirt, showing his smooth skin with hair that led from his stomach to underneath the waistband of his boxers. With both of us in underwear, he stepped into me, allowing his lips to caress my neck as he unclipped my bra, freeing my breasts. The last thing he did was drop to his knees, taking my panties with him. Then he turned me around. "Get your ass on the bed. On all fours."

I did as told and was greeted with a hard slap against my ass cheek. It stung but he rubbed the sting away instantly. I whined when Law slapped my ass again, followed by a delicious squeeze and rub, soothing the pain away. He did the same on the other side and when he stopped, I oddly found myself pushing back to feel more of the same. There was something to this pain and pleasure sensation.

With my feet on the edge of the mattress, he pushed my head downward and pulled my hips higher.

"You fine as fuck," he growled from much lower than I expected. "And you smell good."

I turned around just in time to see his head come close right before his tongue touched my core. I inhaled sharply and squeezed the sheets underneath me. "Oh my, God."

He moaned into me with every lick, enjoying it just as much as me. My head stuffed into the mattress, I could do nothing more than moan with every caress of his tongue on my love. My body took on a mind of its own, pushing back on his face to feel more of everything he had to give.

"Don't stop. Don't stop." I could barely catch my breath. He pushed his solid tongue further into me and I tightened into a ball before exploding all over him, screaming into the mattress.

Law stood and started smacking my ass again. The vibration from it sent aftershocks straight to my bud, magnifying the experience. And again, my God. Sex with Ken had been good, even great, but fuck, Law was doing something to my soul. My legs shook from my hips to the tips of my toes.

"Flip over," he commanded.

I called on all my energy to roll my body over on my back. I was already spent but I knew he was just getting started. He dropped his boxers and ripped open a condom, sliding it over his long shaft. His gruff voice the only sound in the room. "Legs in the air."

My legs straight up, he bent over and I thought he was getting ready for round two of tasting. Instead, he inserted one finger, and then two. "You soaking wet. You must've liked my tongue down there, huh?"

"Yes," I moaned out, my own hands sliding up and down the backs of my thighs.

He moved his fingers in a slow rhythm, then hooked them to find my spot almost immediately. He sped it up, faster and faster, until I was out of breath again. "Tell me what you want."

I wanted to never leave his bed again. After tonight, Law would be lucky if I ever left his place. He pulled out his fingers and licked each one, making sure I was watching. Then he spread my legs into a "V" and rested his dick against my entrance.

"I want you," I whispered.

"What you want from me?" He still didn't move.

"I want you to fuck me, Law."

"Uhmm," he smacked his dick against my opening. "I like when you say my name. Say it again, Shorty."

I wiggled against him and as soon as I said, "Law," he plunged into me, making me scream out. He held us in place as I caught my breath.

"Shit," we said at the same time. I could feel my walls vibrating around him.

"Yeah, that's right." He pulled back out and plunged in again. I pulsed even more. "I knew you liked that."

Instead of going in hard again, he established a nice, slow, tortuous rhythm that built an incredible pressure right before he pulled out and told me, "All fours."

My legs and arms shook on top of the creaky mattress as I assumed the position and moved to the middle of the bed. He came in behind me, slipping back in again and the only sound was him sliding in and out of me. Then he slapped my ass again and the pressure returned, harder this time. I couldn't stop screaming his name, which egged him on.

"What you need, Shorty?"

I tried speaking but sounded like a sex crazed woman who couldn't get one sentence out. "P-please."

He rocked into me faster and laughed. "Please, what? And you better say my name."

"Make me come, Law. Please." I couldn't believe I was begging a man for my own release.

He pushed my head into the mattress and gripped my hips, pulling me deeper into him. Yes, that was it. That was the spot and he knew it. He went harder and faster, the bed rocking like it was moments from breaking into pieces.

"Fuck, you feel so good around this dick." Law groaned out. He reached between my legs and rubbed my clit. I exploded again and he held my hips hostage as he pumped out of control behind me, riding out my orgasm. "Aww fuck, Shorty, I'm coming, too," he said in spurts right before he slammed into me one last time.

With not an ounce of strength left, I collapsed onto the bed after he pulled out to go to the bathroom. The next thing I knew, he was waking me just as the sun was peaking. "Wake up, Shorty."

His hand resting on my hip, I opened my eyes and stretched. My body felt every part of the action it had received last night but waking up to Law was worth it. I snuggled up next to his warm, naked body. He removed the hair from my forehead and supplied a kiss that was just as delicious. His mouth, reminiscent of my smell.

He ended the kiss, and then kissed my neck. "I wish you could stay but I gotta get you home."

I shook my head and kissed his neck in return. "Not yet, Law. One more time."

He moaned and caressed my hip. "That sounds good but my girl gonna be home from work soon so we gotta go."

My eyes flew all the way open and I froze, my hand still on his dick. "Your girl?" I croaked.

Chapter 7

Big Mad

"Why didn't you tell me you had a girlfriend?" I focused on trying to slow down my breathing but underneath the covers, my anger brewed.

Law rolled out the bed and shrugged, tossing me a glance over his shoulder as he pulled on his jeans. "You ain't ask."

I followed behind him and started pulling on my undergarments. Law watched, checking out my figure in the daylight the same way I'd felt all over his during the night. "I didn't ask? I didn't ask! I shouldn't have had to!"

Fully dressed, I stomped back to the bed to look for my hoop earrings that had fallen off during the night. "If you're taking me back to your place to have sex then it's assumed I'm having sex with someone just as single as me! Didn't you ask me if I had a man?" I asked the question more to myself than I did to him, wondering why I hadn't asked if he were in a relationship.

"And where the hell are my earrings?" I flung the sheets back, causing my earrings to fly onto the floor. I quickly scooped them up and locked them into place. The last thing I wanted was to run into the girlfriend. If she handled business in the same manner as it appeared that Law handled his, I needed to get the hell out of there.

Law sat on the pile of clothes on the chair he'd thrown his coat on last night. The pile held bras and more womanly clothing, something I never would've seen in the dark. More items like a head scarf, heels, flat iron, and a cute little leather bomber jacket caught my eye when I finally dared to look around.

"One, never assume shit. Two, to soothe your nerves 'cause you wildin' over there, me and my girl's relationship is complicated, and you don't need to be worried about none of that. Everythang cool." He smiled and damn if I ain't wanna fall back in the bed with him. Law was attractive as hell with his hair wild and free, his chill but gruff voice, and his calm demeanor. And it sure didn't help matters that I knew what he was working with in his pants.

I sighed, "I don't have sex with men in relationships."

He shrugged his shoulders. "A'ight."

I wanted him to say something else like, this was all a joke, or that he would go as far as to break up with his girl, but that wasn't gonna happen. I could not believe my luck, or lack thereof.

Law had put it down so good I didn't know where I was, woke up and still didn't ask, and would skip my happy ass back to him with a smile if he told me he was single. Dick whipped my first night out. Shame. Shame. Shame.

"You got all your shit?" He stood up, preparing to leave. "Y'all women be tryna leave shit behind just to have a reason to come back."

I grabbed my purse and headed to the door. "I'm not them; you ain't gotta worry about that."

"Well, just so you know, you don't need any excuse to see me. You say the word and I'll meet you anywhere, anytime."

"We won't have any more meet ups until you're a single

man." I yanked his front door open and wanted to scream. It had snowed at least four inches overnight. I looked down at my shorts and sneakers and balled up my fists. This was complete bullshit.

Law walked around me and stepped outside. "Want me to carry you?" he winked.

I pushed him out the way, stomping all the way to his car, snow seeping inside my sneakers, freezing my ankles immediately.

He started the car and blasted the heat, handing me his phone. "Put in your address so I know where I'm going."

I did so quietly and pressed navigate. Half a block away, he finally said, "I don't need to explain, but like I said, my relationship is complicated. She probably wasn't even at work last night," he mumbled the last part.

I kept my gaze out the window and wrapped my arms around my body, doing anything to keep warm until the car finished heating up. "So you two just go around cheating on each other? I bet you won't even change the sheets before she lays back in the bed." I waved him off.

"You mad as hell over there," he chuckled, clearly amused. "Why you so mad, Shorty? You wanted me all to yourself?"

My teeth chattered as we rolled to a stop at a stop sign. He removed his large coat and draped it over me. "Even if you do hate me, I can't have you freezing to death," he added with a smile.

I thanked him and sank into the feeling of his coat and his smell around my body again. Law was right, I had wanted him to myself. I shouldn't have, but he was the person I had chosen to give my body to after a bout of celibacy. The fact that we wouldn't be together again in that way was a pity because, baby, my kitty was already missing his cheating ass.

"You type in the right address? It look like this thing got me going to Dunkin Donuts."

"That's where you're taking me." I removed his jacket when we pulled into the parking lot, immediately missing the warmth.

"I'm taking you home after that?" He put the car in park and leaned back to look at me.

"No." My bitter tone left a sour taste in the air. "Go home to your girl and work things out with her. Thanks for the dick."

When I got out the car, he cut off his engine. I heard the crunch of his boots in the snow behind me but I kept walking. "Wait, Shorty. Hold up."

I rolled my eyes, walking as fast as I could to avoid the cold but he caught up to me and blocked the entrance.

"Aye, I don't want you to leave like this."

I shivered and yet again, he wrapped his coat around my shoulders. "Here. Keep it this time. It'll at least keep you warm until you make it home." He glanced around the parking lot. "And it'll keep all these mutha fuckas from staring at your ass."

"Law," I shook my head.

"I ain't mean to hurt you like this, Shorty. Like I said, I was the luckiest nigga because you went home with me. I still feel that way even if you mad. Tell me how to make you smile again."

"Just leave it alone."

"Can't do that. Let me see," he took a step back and brought his fist to his chin as if in deep thought. "You want me to buy you something? What you want? Roses? One of them Telfar bags? I can't get you jewelry; we ain't there yet."

A smile started on my face and Law saw it. "There's that smile I remember. You want me to beg for forgiveness, don't you?"

He kneeled down as if he were completely oblivious to the snow. "Law, get up."

"Naw, I ain't doing that until you forgive me." He looked up at me. "Hey, I'm sorry for misleading you." He palmed the sides of my thighs. "You forgive me?"

Him on his knees, in front of me with those bedroom eyes, was taking me places I had no business going so I pushed my needs to the side, a habit I was fairly good at doing. "If I say yes, will you get up and let me be on my way?"

"Can't make no promises." He bit his bottom lip and his eyes traveled to my legs and back up to my face. "I know what you want. You want my face back in between those thighs, don't you?"

"Law," I gasped. "I can't believe you just said that." My eyes quickly scanned the area to see if anyone was around to hear him. Other than two women walking through the doors of the restaurant, we were alone.

His hands grabbed my rear. "Want me to spank you, again?" When he added a squeeze, my eyes involuntarily closed. "I don't want you to be upset, Shorty. No one as beautiful as you should ever be mad."

I mentally counted to three and responded, "I'm not upset anymore."

He stood up and I immediately missed the physical contact but this was for the best. "You promise?"

"Yeah, I'm good. Thank you for last night."

He stared at me for a moment and pulled a hundred dollars out, stuffing it into my palm. "Use this for breakfast and a ride since you don't want me knowing where you live. Text me when you get home." He kissed my lips and palmed my face. "See you later, Shorty."

I walked into Dunkin Donuts, overthinking my feelings and the situation, when I realized I was still in his coat. Even though he said to keep it, I hadn't actually meant to. We surely didn't need any other reason to see each other.

After I placed my order, I called Nisha. "Come get me," I hissed.

"Huh?" she asked, her voice filled with sleep.

"Law had to drop me off somewhere because his girlfriend, that I had no idea existed, was on her way home. I'm stranded and since this was all your idea, you get to pick me up and take me home."

"Girl, I'm tired. Call an Uber or something."

"Come get me Nish!" I gave her the address and hung up. Right as I was putting away my phone it buzzed with a text.

Good morning beautiful

I counted to three again and sighed. What a fucking weekend.

Chapter 8

Socks

I DIDN'T HAVE THE MENTAL CAPACITY TO DEAL WITH ISAIAH'S good morning text. All I wanted was to get home and relax into a bubble bath that would ease the ache in my head and the one in between my thighs. Every time I thought about my circumstances, chilled goosebumps perked up on my arms and my toes curled against each other in my shoes. My body had the nerve to be sexually pleased and frustrated at the same damn time.

When a shiver ran up my spine I squeezed my coffee cup, causing the lid to pop off.

"Ouch!" The coffee trickled down the side of the cup and into my palm. I stuffed my donut into my mouth so I could have a free hand to press the lid back onto my coffee cup.

Turning around to grab a napkin, I stopped in my tracks. My new boss, Mr. Ward, was standing in line to get some grub; the same new boss I was due to start working for tomorrow morning. And I was standing there wearing teenie shorts, a belly shirt, a coat that clearly wasn't mine, and I had a donut hanging out my mouth. Totally not the impression I wanted to share right before my first day.

Standing there frozen, I debated how to get out of there without being noticed. Just then, the half of my donut hanging out my mouth started to bend until it finally fell to the floor with a loud plop. I quickly turned my back to Mr. Ward right as he looked up. Please God, let him not have seen my face.

As fast as I could, I walked my ass to the bathroom to hideout and clean off my hands. Hopefully, by the time I was done, Mr. Ward would be gone and I could pester Nisha about how much longer I'd have to wait for her.

I shook my head as I removed the heat protectant sleeve and rinsed the coffee from the outside of my cup. I should've just stayed home when Nisha asked me to go out with her last night. I'd already seen my ex-husband, had a spat with a new lover, run into my boss, and been stranded at a Dunkin Donuts.

Standing against the wall, my eyes toward the ceiling, I realized that booty calls could not and would not be my thing. I needed and deserved more stability. Maybe that meant entertaining the idea of having a boyfriend and maybe that meant I had a few friends. Either way, nights like what I'd just had weren't it for me.

Here

Nisha's text sent my phone buzzing.

Be right out

I tapped onto my screen.

I tucked my extra donuts under my arm and cracked the bathroom door, peeking for signs of Mr. Ward. With the coast clear, I tiptoed down the brightly lit hallway. When I got to the end, I peered around the wall. Mr. Ward was now standing on the side waiting for his order. As long as I didn't make a scene, I was in the clear.

Pulling Law's coat up and over the back of my head, I made my way to the door, holding my breath the entire way. When I got to the double doors, I ran the rest of the way with the extra donuts and jumped in Nisha's car. "Go!"

"Girl, what's wrong?" Mouth agape, eyes squinted, Nisha screamed, "Is someone after you?"

"Just go! And hurry up!"

Nisha stepped on the gas, her tires spinning in the snow. "Why do you have me peeling out of here like you stole something? What's going on?" She took a deep breath. "You got my heart racing all fast. It's too early for this."

"My boss was in there and I didn't want him seeing me like this."

Nisha looked at me, blinked twice, looked back at the road, and then back to me. "Your boss? Are you kidding me right now?"

"No," I whined and reclined the seat to a more comfortable position. "This entire morning has been a nightmare thanks to you." I pinched her thigh and ignored my ringing phone.

"Oww," she smacked my hand and tried to pinch me back. "You really out here running away from your boss? I thought you were getting trafficked or something! And what's this about a nightmare?"

"I can't have my boss see me like this. I need this job. And yes, I'm still waiting to wake up from my nightmare so let's talk about why you had to pick me up." I smacked her bicep with the back of my hand.

"Sync! How could I have known Law had a girlfriend? From the looks of it you don't seem to care too much. You wearing his coat like y'all in high school and it's his letterman."

"Don't change the subject."

"Like I said, I didn't know. My bad, Girl." Nisha was quiet for a minute, but then she whispered with a guilty smile on her face. "Were my instincts right? Was it good?"

Arms crossed, I looked at her and she shrugged. A well burst inside of me and I covered my blushing face. "I thought you'd never ask, Nisha," I gushed.

"Damn! It was like that?"

"I can't even lie, that might've been the best dick I ever had."

"Girl!" Nisha hit her steering wheel repeatedly with her palm. "I knew it! I knew it!"

"I almost wanted to cry."

"You might have to double back to that then."

"I can't, Nisha. He has a girlfriend."

"Oh yeah. Are they serious, though?"

"I won't be that girl. I can't."

"Well, too bad about her but I'm glad you finally got some. You know you gonna have to tell me the details. I need to know what positions he had you in, how many times you came, how big he was...Do you feel less stressed?" she added as an afterthought and then giggled like a kid discovering a water slide for the first time.

"I don't know. I would feel less stressed if I didn't sleep with somebody's man."

"Listen, you didn't know he was with someone so don't let it get to you. For real, for real, you'll probably never hear from him again unless you come back to the rink with me."

"Bet you're right. From what I could tell, he cheats on her all the time." My phone buzzed with a text message so I pulled my phone back out of my bag.

An image of my knee-high socks lit up the screen.

You left your socks Shorty.

Chapter 9

Same Ol' Same Ol'

"HAVE A GOOD DAY," I NODDED TO THE CITY BUS DRIVER AND stepped onto the sidewalk that lined the exterior of my new office building. The cold air whipped against my face, forcing me to pull my vegan suede trench coat tighter to avoid the rest of my body freezing up. I briskly walked the rest of the way, needing to get inside the warmth as fast as possible.

As soon as I walked into the building, I had to step to the side to answer my phone. This was the second time Ken had called but I still didn't have the energy to deal with the conversation that was due. Not just because he had questions that I didn't have answers to, but because I just couldn't. At least, not right now. And probably not tomorrow or the day after, but soon. I'd call him soon.

I stepped back in with the flow of people hustling to the elevator to get their days started. They ranged from those with tightly pulled scarves warming their brains and bodies with coffee, and those with scowls on their faces. I wanted to be happy I was here but I felt more in tune with those with the scowls. As happy as I was to get my coins back to a good place, I hated that I needed this job. Since my accident, I'd blown through a hefty size of my savings to cover the bills that kept coming in; bill collectors were ruthless. Originally I had over twenty-five thousand and now I barely had enough to pay rent for the next two months.

But such is life. Honestly, my new job didn't seem to be too bad from what I gathered from the interview. I could arrive anytime between six and nine and leave after I completed eight hours of work. The kicker was that after I got a handle on my work, I'd be able to request to work from home for up to two days a week. Working in my pajamas with a glass of wine sounded right up my alley.

"Good morning, Amber." One of my new bosses, Ryann, caught up to me right outside the elevator. She was the one who interviewed me and was actually quite pleasant. In total, I had three bosses. Ryann, Mr. Ward, who I ran from yesterday, and Mr. O'Brien. They were all part owner of the human resources firm with Mr. O'Brien holding majority.

Ryann smiled and pressed the up arrow. "You're early, that's good. When we get upstairs I'll show you to your desk, let you unpack, and then show you around. First days are always the longest so be prepared."

All I could do was smile and nod. Little did she know, the day already felt long.

Even in the dead of winter, Ryann reeked of money with her maroon lipstick, what looked to be a cashmere coat with a thin belt, a purse with lots of bling and a smooth leather surface, and high heels that didn't appear to have ever touched the ground.

We'd just arrived at my desk, right in the middle of the floor, when Ryann's attention was pulled away. She was looking so long that I had to turn around. "Good morning, Mr. Ward. You remember Amber? Our new admin assistant? Today is her first day."

If he recognized me from Dunkin Donuts, he didn't say

anything, but I continued holding my breath as I took in everything that he was. Mr. Ward was a handsome man. Not my type, but handsome, nonetheless. He was probably somewhere in his fifties and I would bet my last dollar that he could pull women in every age bracket.

He held out his hand to shake, which I took. As clean cut as he was, the calluses were a nice surprise. "Yes, I remember you. Welcome aboard, glad to have you here."

"Happy to be here." He released my hand, allowing it to slide out like he didn't want to let it go. Or was I imagining things? Every man I saw brought me right back to memories of what I shared with Law. He'd opened my sexual floodgates and now I was horny as hell. My body craved more.

"Ryann is a wonderful trainer and will have you up to speed in no time," Mr. Ward intruded into my thoughts.

Ryann giggled like she was at a comedy show. Were they an item? Did she want them to be? If she wanted to dip her toe into Mr. Ward's pool, I couldn't blame her. Everything about him screamed sex appeal. Dressed in a plain powder blue dress shirt with the top button open, no tie, a suit jacket with matching slacks, and his cologne as its own accessory, he had to know every woman's head turned when he sailed by.

I fixed my lips to express the first lie of many that I undoubtedly, knew I'd tell today. "I look forward to getting up to speed."

"Happy to hear that." He turned to Ryann. "What do you have planned for Amber today?"

Ryann went into an explanation about the day. I should've been listening but I wanted to check out Mr. Ward again. His arms over his chest, he listened, nodding when necessary, but then his gaze drifted to me once. And then again. Unlike the looks I'd received from Ken and Law, Mr. Ward wasn't assessing my appearance. It felt more like he was trying to place where he'd seen me and I wanted to die on the spot. They say a guilty conscience will tell on you every time and I had a feeling that my fidgety foot was going to blow up my spot.

Needing to do something, I interrupted Ryann, "This all sounds like a lot, but I know I can handle it."

Mr. Ward cleared his throat and tapped Ryann on her upper arm. "Wonderful, Amber. Ryann, I don't mean to cut this short but I have a meeting to prep for. Let me know if you need anything. You ladies have a good day."

Once Mr. Ward was out of earshot, Ryann's smile faded. "As one of the owners of this firm, you will never interrupt me again. Understood?"

"One hundred percent." Maybe my pleasant perception of her hadn't been correct. If she was like this every day I'd be searching for a new position before the end of the week.

By midafternoon my feet were killing me and my stomach was protesting the lack of food I'd stuffed into it. Being in the office all day instead of at home was going to be an adjustment for my mind, and my belly.

"Alright, let's pause here." Ryann, who didn't appear to be even a little bit fatigued, stood up from my desk. "You get forty-five minutes for lunch so let's meet back up here around one-thirty."

I walked into the breakroom and was elated to see another employee. And not just any employee, a sistah who appeared to be about my age. She seemed cool enough, but I'd already misinterpreted one person's personality; I'd be cautious with this one. Plus, she was on the phone and it sounded like she was trying to keep the person from plunging off the deep end. I couldn't help but eavesdrop as I microwaved my leftovers from my dinner and mimosas with Nisha.

"I know and you know he ain't no good. I been told you to leave him."

Yikes. She had to be on the phone with one of her friends. I, too, had talked my friends through situations like this and that was one of the reasons I knew I couldn't see Law again. At least, not until he was single.

"How much more evidence do you need?" She set her Chinese takeout down and plopped into a chair. "You found what? Some socks?"

My mind immediately flashed to the last text I'd gotten from Law.

"What kind of socks? Are you sure they weren't yours?" She stuffed more food in her mouth and then asked, "And what did Law say?"

My hand on the microwave handle, I froze in place. She couldn't have said what I thought she said. I opened the microwave as quietly as possible without looking suspicious. I needed to hear more of the conversation.

"He said what? That he bought them for you? Weren't they already worn?"

Right then, I heard the woman's voice. It was muffled but she'd started yelling and I heard everything I needed to. "What I look like wearing long ass black socks? Law think I'm a fool. I bet he met whoever she was down at that busted ass skating rink."

Before my food could finish heating, I grabbed it and walked back to my desk as fast as I could. I was not starting my new job search this weekend, I was starting it now.

Chapter 10

Parked

By Friday I'd stopped absorbing every bit of the information Ryann had shoved into my face throughout the week. And I'd also successfully avoided Law's girlfriend's friend. I didn't need any new friends anyway.

Each day, I'd learned several new reports and on this Friday, I couldn't take anymore. There was a report for everything and there was always paperwork to complete for some sexual harassment or insurance claim, a new hire, or a fire.

My other duties had me following up with clients, taking notes, assisting with timesheets, and acting as the liaison between the employees and the professional department. Basically, it was too much work for one person but I needed this job, so I was stuck, at least for now.

"Once you find your flow, it'll be a cakewalk. Next week I'll be around for questions but after that you're on your own. None of us have time to babysit." Ryann gestured to the offices of Mr. Ward and Mr. O'Brien.

"Okay." A tight smile graced my face. Ryann was turning out to be my least favorite person. I had started my job search again but was determined to not quit until I had an offer from a different company.

"Since we finished early, we'll stop here and you can take a longer lunch. For the second half of the day you'll be with Mr. Ward. He'll walk you around and introduce you to the department supervisors." She closed her laptop at my desk. "Go directly to his office when you return. Don't be late."

When I was sure she had returned to her office, I pulled out my cell. Keeping my voice low, my fingers quaked as I tapped in the numbers. I had no business doing this. Next to my suicide attempt, it was probably the worst decision I'd made, but this week had stressed me out so bad and I needed to leave it all behind, even if only during my lunch.

Hey, my training ended early so I'm ready earlier than expected.

Good 'cause I'm already here.

Just his voice made me more anxious. Anxious to see him. Anxious to know whether he'd touch me. Just plain ol' anxious to be in his presence.

"You parked where I told you to?"

"Yeah. Now bring your fine ass out here."

I hung up the phone with a quickness. Halfway to the door, a text came through.

Take your panties off b4u come down here

Shivers ran up my spine and back down again. I had to pull it together. I responded back,

Not happening

He sent a smirking emoji back and my grip tightened on my phone. Whatever it was about him that made me so damn horny, I needed it to dissolve. As best I could, I pep talked the shit out of myself on the elevator ride down. I had called him for one reason-my socks. He was returning my socks. That was it. That was all.

But if I were completely honest with myself, I ain't even need them socks. I was poor, at the moment, but not so poor that I couldn't afford to replace a pair of socks that I never wore anyway. I knew I had contacted him because even though he was off the market, he made me feel special. And adored. Selfish or not, I needed that. Plus, nothing more would happen except maybe some flirting and conversation. I could handle that.

Stepping onto the chilled pavement, I looked for his car but didn't see it. My phone buzzed.

> Keep walking all the way to the back. Black Accord

I spotted him in the far rear under the bare, snow-covered trees. No other cars were around and although it looked odd to be the only car back there, no one here would give it a second look.

I climbed inside his car and flashbacks of us chilled me more than the wind rocking the car. His delicious scent sucked me in first, urging me to jump into his arms. His accent that I hadn't been able to place, pulled me in even further.

"Hey, Shorty."

The smile on Law's face caused a tingle between my legs that wet my panties. I was in trouble. But I'd known that when I sent that first text that apologized for leaving my socks at his place. I'd also known that when I sent the subsequent text that requested him to bring them to me.

"Hey, Law."

"Why you ain't never wearing a coat?" He sat back on a lean, with the driver side door supporting his frame. He spoke directly to me but kept his gaze on my chest, his low eyes tracing the outline of my breasts inside my white form fitting sweater.

And me? I couldn't move my eyes from those juicy lips. The ones that had kissed my feminine areas and brought me to orgasm multiple times. My nipples peaked at the memory.

"Was just planning on running down."

He reached for my hand, using his thumb to stroke the inside of my palm. My sight followed his hand along my skin while his warm touch lit fires up and down my arms. Fires that I didn't want to be put out.

He adjusted in his seat and brought my hand to his mouth, kissing the inside of my wrist. "What else was you planning on?"

"Just to get my socks." My voice, hoarse all of a sudden, matched his.

He released my hand and slowly pulled my socks from his coat pocket, holding them in the air. A challenge. If I'd come specifically for the socks then I needed to grab them and get back in the office. That was the best course of action. It should've been my only course of action.

But I stared at them, unable to stuff them into my hands because that meant our time would end. I'd go back to the job I hated and not have contact with Law again. That wasn't what I wanted.

He smirked and placed my socks on his dashboard. If I was going to leave this car before something happened, I needed to do it now. Once he kissed me, as I knew he would, I wouldn't be able to walk away.

Law linked his lanky fingers with mine, pulling me over the center console and into his arms. Right before our lips touched, he whispered, "Missed you."

Chapter 11

Something About Law

I'D FALLEN RIGHT INTO MY OWN TRAP AND ONTO LAW'S LIPS. HIS mouth gently brushed against my top lip, his breath light against my skin. Like they were on their own accord they lingered as if trying to decide whether I was worth the taste. I could assure him that I was. Without. A. Doubt. He proved he knew as much by tilting his head and using his hand behind my neck to keep me close. He dove in, moving to suck my bottom lip before drawing my tongue into his mouth.

In my past, Law wasn't someone I would've been attracted to. If we'd seen each other in passing, neither of us would have given the other a second glance. But since I'd become Sync, my world had shifted, allowing Law to skate right into my life. It had barely been a week since I'd last laid in his bed and my pussy was calling out to him like he'd stamped it forever his, with love.

My skirt wrapped around my waist, my tights sufficiently soaked, I grinded on top of him, trying to cure the ache that continued building. I moaned from the friction. Whatever we were going to do in this car, I was determined to get mine even if he didn't get his.

Law and I didn't belong to each other, meaning that after this moment in his car, there was no guarantee we'd see each other's faces again. I'd find someone after him, that wasn't a question, but it wouldn't be another Law. I still hadn't officially talked to Isaiah but...

Inadvertently, my lips had stopped moving, making Law open his eyes. Tugging on my lip, he slowly pulled away. "You good?"

"Yeah." And I was ready for Law to make me forget about Isaiah the same way he'd made me forget about Ken. I went for his neck but he stalled me.

"Wait," he whispered, his eyes focused on the parking lot. "Someone walking by."

I turned around to see Ryann walking between a row of cars. "Dammit!"

I tried ducking but he wouldn't let me. He just chuckled. "They can't see in here. We can only see out."

"Right," I whispered.

"Tints." His mouth smacked against the dip above my collar bone. "She'll be gone in a minute."

"Yeah." I came down from the high that was Law. For some odd reason, I trusted him when he said Ryann couldn't see us. But what about security cameras? What if his girlfriend's friend came out and saw his car? I was in the parking lot of a job that I needed to keep. I couldn't afford any trouble when I was still on probation. "Law, I can't do this."

His kisses slowed until they eventually ended with him looking at me. "That's your choice."

"I'm sorry."

"You ain't gotta apologize. I get it."

Many words were left unsaid in my heart. What left my mouth were, "...my job."

His hands rubbed up and down my back, continued down my thighs, and stopped at my knees that planked his sides.

Tension that built throughout the week dissipated through a released sigh that left my forehead against his.

"We can just sit, if that's what you want."

I wanted more than to sit on his lap. I wanted to not go back up to my desk with an attitude fueled by sexual frustration. I wanted to not be in a situation where I was forced to choose. I wanted-more.

Law's hands traced lines from my wrists to the inside of my elbows. I shuddered from his touch and when I opened my eyes back up, his bottom lip was tucked between his teeth. His hooded eyes knew I wanted him.

I ran my fingers up and down his neck. Slowly, from the bottoms of his ears to the top of his coat collar. His chestnut-colored skin begged me to taste him. There was something about Law that I adored. Something that drew me to him. Something in his eyes that beckoned me closer each time he was around.

The decision I needed to make lingered. Law? Or my job? I needed my job but I also needed Law right now. However, I'd already started my job search so it wouldn't be long before I had another offer. Plus, as a last resort, I still had money in my account. Enough to get me through if there was an emergency until I found a new job.

But all that depended on me actually being fired. There was no guarantee that we'd be caught. Cameras couldn't see through tints just as people couldn't. Right?

Nostrils flaring, Law pressed his massive length against my clothed bottom, thrusting up. "Is that what you want?"

With our chests together, I felt when his rib cage expanded more deeply. Knowing how much he wanted me, how much he was struggling to keep it together, made me want him more. Why did he want me so bad? Why did he believe I was so valuable? Worthy? Sexy.

I leaned down and whispered into his neck. "I want you."

His voice cracked when my tongue licked a line to the bottom of his ear. "Say less."

In the tight confines of the car, he rushed me out of one leg of my tights. Then helped that same leg out of my panties. I pulled his jeans down his hips just enough for his dick to spring free. I'd sucked enough dicks in my life, just because I'd felt like I needed to return the favor. But Law's dick? I wanted to taste him so bad. Make him forget how to talk. Watch his eyes roll back into his head.

His hands rolled the condom down and guided me onto the tip. I wanted to say I'd forgotten how he felt but it'd been all I could think about. And now I was about to slide into bliss. I grabbed his shoulders for support, slowly adjusting to his size and feel.

I was about halfway down when Law groaned like he was losing his mind and pulled me all the way onto him, causing both of us to gasp. He squeezed my ass and coaxed me up and down, setting the torturous, slow pace. Law was every bit of the definition of sex.

I couldn't catch my breath. My fingers squeezed his shoulders for dear life. I wished I could be naked on top of him, riding him in his bed, but I had to take what I could get. And right now, Law was giving it, bouncing me all around his car.

Each time I slid down, he pushed up deeper into me. We'd just started and I already felt like I was going to burst. A feeling that Law must have felt too.

"Hell yeah. You missed this dick didn't you?"

"Yes. Yes." My head hung backwards, my chest pushed forwards, I noticed the windows starting to fog up.

"Yes, what? Say my name, Shorty." He thrust into me deeper. "Don't act like you forgot."

"Law, yes. Yes, Law." In the confines of the car he held all the moves in his hips. It was like we were back in his bed. The car rocked as Law chased the release I was due. It was right on the tip of my...my, "LAW!"

My insides tightened into a ball and I screamed louder than ever. The wetness underneath me had me looking down and I prayed Law hadn't somehow jumpstarted my period, if that was a thing.

Law pulled up my skirt, his mouth curving up on one side when he saw what had happened. "Damn baby."

I balled the skirt in my hands and followed his gaze. A small pool of liquid flowed over the side of his legs and onto his seat. That hadn't happened before but shit, it felt so good I wanted it to happen again. I started riding him again. Same speed. Same stroke. Same angle. The tension immediately built back up.

He watched as my eyes fluttered shut. I leaned backwards, my moans filling the rocking car. I rolled my hips all over his dick, grabbing his hair and pulling his head down to my breasts.

"That's it. Take that dick, Shorty." The sound of our bodies joining vibrated against the windows. The sounds so erotic that I came again, this time, gushing even more. I swear I saw stars this time.

Law's lips smacked against the underside of my chin, his arms holding my limp body tightly. "You ain't tell me you was a squirter."

I shook my head, barely able to lift it. "I didn't know."

He pulled away to gaze at me. "That never happened before?"

"No," I breathed into the window.

He pulled me closer and bit my bottom lip. "That's sexy as hell." His hands found my waist and started moving me again. "My turn. Kiss my neck."

Not only did I kiss it, but I licked, sucked, and ran my tongue up and down like it was his dick.

"Hell yeah. Just like that. Don't stop, Shorty." Our bodies

picked up speed, slamming into each other. I didn't know who was fucking who but I screamed his name again as my body released for the third time. Law came seconds after, fingers squeezing so hard he left divots in my sides.

Curled into his arms, our breathing returning to normal, Law reached around me to pull napkins from the glove compartment. I took that opportunity to climb back into my seat and pull my panties and tights back on.

I checked the clock. We'd been in here longer than I realized and I still needed to dash to the restroom to clean off before I met with Mr. Ward. There was no way I could go in his office smelling like condoms and pussy.

Law looked up from buckling his belt. "Coming to the rink tomorrow?"

Tempting. But no. As irrational as it seemed, I couldn't just see him on the regular without a reason. He belonged to another woman and I needed to remember that. "I have errands to run."

He nodded slowly, like he didn't believe me. I wouldn't have believed me either. I'd never been a good liar. "A'ight. Gotta get back upstairs?"

"Yeah." My hand on the handle, he grabbed my other wrist. When I turned around he brought our mouths together. Long and hard. Like he was trying to convince me that he was worth another visit, as I'd wanted to convince him earlier.

He ended the kiss, to my dismay, and grabbed my socks from the dashboard, holding them out for me. I stared at the socks before balling them into my fist. This symbolized the end. I had what I'd asked him to bring. There was no other reason to meet. This. Was. It.

I started to get out, but again, he stopped me. "When you giving me my coat back?"

His coat. I'd forgotten about that and now I had another excuse to see him. It shouldn't have excited me but a smile made its way onto my face. Law returned it with a smile of his own.

"Monday?" he suggested.

"Sure. I'll bring it to work on Monday."

"Good. Bye, Shorty."

"Bye Law." I exited his car and booked it back upstairs, making it to Mr. Ward's office with one minute to spare.

Chapter 12

Hey Ken

I laid in my bed until almost noon, reliving every moment between Law and I during our time in his car. He'd whispered that he missed me in the heat of the moment. I'm not saying I believed him, but I believed that he believed it.

Afterwards, we had texted throughout the rest of my workday and video chatted well into the morning after I got home. For my sake, I knew I needed to keep it to sex only but Law was making it hard to not like him.

The only thing keeping the smile off my face was the number of times that Ken had hit me up already this morning. His calls had started a couple of hours ago and I was beginning to think something was wrong. He wasn't the type to call back-to-back and now he was texting me.

Please answer 911

He sent another text.

Need your help. Don't have anyone else. We don't gotta talk about our divorce

I gave in and called him back. Not surprisingly, he answered on the first ring.

"I was beginning to think you gave me the wrong number." Ken added a short awkward laugh but I didn't respond to his comment. Whatever I said would ultimately be the wrong thing.

"What's going on?" I asked. "Are you okay?"

"Well, I'm not on my death bed or anything like that but I am in a bind. I was playing tennis with a buddy of mine this morning and I tripped. My friend drove me to the hospital and it turns out that I broke my foot so I can't drive. My car is still at the club and..."

I immediately knew where this was going. "I see uh, you broke your left foot?"

"Yeah."

To make sure we were on the same page, I asked, "What exactly are you asking me to help with?"

"I'm asking if you can pick me up from the hospital and drive me to my car? From there, you drive my car back to my place and I'll drive yours. Then you can get back to your day. Is that something you can help me with?"

Yep, exactly what I'd assumed. Ken's car was his prized possession. It was his wife. And it had cost almost as much as our four-bedroom suburban house at the time. He loved his Porsche 911 and had taught me how to drive the stick shift as soon as he pulled it off the dealer's lot. Learning how to drive with both feet had been a struggle but he'd been patient and had cheered me on when I finally got the hang of it. His father was the only person I knew of that could also drive one but he'd passed away years ago.

"There's no one else?" I asked, already knowing the answer.

"Unfortunately, not."

"What about your friend that you were playing tennis with?"

"He was the first one I asked."

"And your, umm, lady friend from the rink?"

"She hasn't earned that privilege so I didn't ask." What he didn't say, that I still held that honor, kept both of us silent for a moment. "I'm sorry for bothering you but I really don't have anyone else. I figured I'd ask you before I had to splurge on a tow truck. If you can't or don't want to help, I understand."

"It's fine. I'll be there."

"Thank you, Amber. I appreciate this."

"No problem. What hospital are you at?" He gave the address and thirty minutes later I'd thrown on some clothes, unwrapped my hair, bypassed makeup, and was on my way to save the day.

Outside of his room, I heard his voice. And then his laugh. My stomach fluttered with nerves. I hadn't spent significant time with him since I'd left him at the airport and though he said we wouldn't be talking about that, anxiety from our unsaid words floated through my veins.

I meekly drew back the curtain and peeked my head around. "Hey, Ken."

He paused his conversation with his friend and his Adam's apple bobbed when he saw me. The energy in the room cracked as Ken's gaze ate me up. It was the same stare he'd given when he last saw me and I wanted to shrink away. It's not like I was wearing anything revealing; everything was left to the imagination. I was fully covered and comfortable in my grey and black leggings, an old Myrtle Beach sweatshirt, and my jean jacket. Since it was unseasonably warm in January at almost forty-five degrees, I'd taken full advantage of not having to wear my puffer coat. Now that I thought of it, that's probably why Ken had driven his Porsche today.

"Hey, Amber."

"Ready to go?"

"Not yet," he swallowed again. "Waiting on the nurse to

bring my discharge papers. Should be soon. You're not in a rush are you?"

"Not at all."

His friend rose from the only chair in the room. "You can sit here."

"Thanks."

That prompted Ken to officially introduce us. "Amber, this is Colten. Colten, this is Amber."

I grabbed his outstretched hand as we traded places. "Nice to meet you."

He nodded. "Likewise."

Before sitting, I stopped at Ken's swollen, propped up foot. "Looks painful. Will they put you in a cast?"

"They said I have to wait for the swelling to go down." He waited a beat before adding, "Thanks again for coming."

Right then, the nurse returned with the discharge papers. "Here are your instructions. Basically, ice the affected area, stay off it, keep it elevated, and take your medicine. When you're home, having everything you need within reach will work wonders for healing. Do you have someone at home to help you?"

Ken glanced at me, the papers the nurse still held, and then back at the nurse. "No, but I'll be fine."

The nurse turned to Colten and me. "Will one of you be able to help Mr. Green get settled at home? Make sure he picks up his medicine before he's left on his own?"

Colten spoke up first. "I actually have to leave now to take my kids to their ice skating lessons but I can swing by later this evening."

"That's cool. Thanks man." They said their goodbyes and bumped fists.

The nurse looked at me next. "How about you?"

Backed into a corner, I didn't have much of a choice. "Sure, I'll help."

"Alright then," the nurse smiled widely to a relieved Ken.

Before releasing him, she adjusted his crutches, making sure he knew how to use them before getting him settled into the waiting wheelchair. "Let's get you out of here so you can get home and rest."

When I pulled my car to the curb, Ken gingerly eased into the passenger seat and I slid his crutches into my back seat before hopping behind the wheel. As a guy that never got sick, never took a day off, and worked through all issues, I felt bad that he was in so much pain.

"Is your car at the same club you used to go to?" I asked before pulling off.

"Yeah."

We endured an awkward silence until he said, "I see you're still driving the Jetta but in a different color. Your old one finally die on you?"

If only he knew. "Yeah, you could say that."

He nodded. I knew he wanted me to be more conversational, but I wasn't in the head space for all that. I had looked forward to enjoying the rest of my day on my couch while catching up on beach side dating shows. I might have even munched on tacos and overpriced wine for dinner in an effort to keep my tryst with Law off my mind. Now I was most likely going to be spending the rest of the day with my ex-husband, which definitely wasn't something I could have predicted.

"Not much has changed in the vehicle department but your looks certainly have."

I shot him the ugliest glare, twisting my neck toward him. "What do you mean by that?"

He held up his hands in surrender. "In a good way. In a good way is what I meant. I like your hair cut and the way you dress now. Like from the rink. It's more revealing-more provocative, but the new look suits you." He paused, but then asked, "Why did you decide to change it up?"

I'd had the same look our entire marriage. Mostly I'd worn earth tones, mascara occasionally, and my long hair had always been in a ponytail at the nape of my neck. Changing it up had been on a whim after my accident but I didn't want him to know the hell I'd survived after we went our separate ways. "It just felt right."

He adjusted in his seat, turning to look at me with his eyes glazed over. "I like the new you. It *does* feel right."

Chapter 13

Backpedal

KEN WAS GOOD FOR SLIPPING IN SUGGESTIVE COMMENTS. Comments that, if questioned, could mean nothing. Or, it could also mean absolutely everything. A smile came over my face because I loved that about him. Or at least, I used to love that about him. No, check that, I still loved that about him. And I loved the suggestive smile that would cross his face right after he said something like that.

Those statements had often led to a raised eyebrow on my face, followed by a subtle head nod by him that beckoned me to him across our sofa or in our bed. Sweet moments where we'd lie together, him rubbing his fingers across my back while we binge watched a series. His lips gracing my forehead lovingly as I snuggled deeper into his arms.

He cleared his throat. "Make a right at the light."

"I remember." I swallowed the lump that had formed in my throat and tried focusing all my attention on the road. Being around him felt like what I hadn't realized I had been missing. If I was halfway truthful with myself, it's the companionship void I'd been using Law to fill. I wasn't a complete idiot. I understood Law would never be mine. He belonged to another woman and even if they broke up, my gut told me he would still belong to the streets.

I chanced a quick glance at Ken. Damn, he was fine. The kind of fine that included knowing you wouldn't have to worry about a thing. I missed not having to stress about finances. I missed being able to order takeout or have food delivered at will. I missed my two-income home and wondered if he missed it too. Still, the question remained, did I miss him or what he provided?

The scenery turned to a street lined with towering trees that flanked the curb, followed by enormous houses with unnecessarily long driveways. I pulled into the parking lot of the club and idled my car next to his Porsche. Holding out my palm, I said, "Alright, hand over your keys and I'll follow you to your place."

"Right." He dug in his pocket. "I forgot you don't have the spare."

"Didn't need it anymore."

"Right." He placed them in my hand, allowing his hand to sit in mine. "Be careful..."

"Ken," I held a warning in my eyes. "I know how to drive your car."

He chuckled, a fresh light in his eyes. "I know, but I also know how you are every time you get into the driver's seat."

We both laughed because he was right. "Why have a Porsche if you're not gonna speed."

"...if you're not gonna speed," he finished the sentence with me, leaving us in a comfortable silence.

"Umm, do you need help getting into the driver's seat?" I asked.

"No," he cleared his throat, "I can manage."

I made my way to his car and started it up, listening to the engine roar to life. Ken slowly hobbled his way around my car to the driver's side. Right before he got in, and just because I used to love pushing his buttons when it came to his precious Porsche, I pushed down on the accelerator and revved the engine. He glared at me over the top of my car, to which I waved back like a princess. His facial features relaxed until he broke out into a smile and laughed. And just like that, we started slipping right back into our old routine.

So when my phone automatically connected to his Porsche, I didn't think twice about why he'd never cleared my phone from the Bluetooth memory. When I couldn't stop smiling while following him to his place, I didn't think twice. Even when I thought about picking him up a bag of chips because even though they were his favorite snack, he always forgot to grab them when he went to the grocery store, I didn't think twice.

Not even Nisha's screeching over the car's speakers ruined the vibe. "You're on your way where?"

My hands gripped the steering wheel. "I am not repeating myself because I know you heard me."

"Then you know why I'm confused. I'm looking at the text you sent me late last night that says you fucked Law in the parking lot at your new job and now you're headed to Ken's place. Are you gonna fuck him too? I suggested you have a one-night stand, not fall in love with a hood nigga and fall back in love with your ex-husband at the same damn time."

"It's not like how you're making it sound, Nisha."

Nisha sighed, long and too loud. "Explain it then, Sync. Because, to me, it sounds like you're spiraling back into the same type of shit that you worked so hard to get out of."

My mouth fell open. "Nisha! Why would you say that?"

"Because I love you, Sync, and something about this doesn't feel right," her voice cracked. "When I saw you spiraling before, I didn't say anything and what happened? You tried to commit suicide. Thank God it didn't work but I haven't stopped blaming myself since then. You were lonely then and I understood why. You're lonely now and I understand why. I get it, Sync. I do.

"When I suggested that you have a roll in the sheets with Law it was because I figured he wasn't the type that would double back. But now it seems like you're in some kind of situationship with him and the morning after, you're on your way to Ken's fucking house! The same Ken that you left at the airport.

"I know you and it feels like you're going down a road where you'll get your heart broken by not one man, but two. That's something that would crush you and in your sensitive state, you don't need anything that will upset the delicate balance and harmony that you've found and created."

As I processed her words I found that I couldn't form my own. Was she right? Was I spiraling? Had I not even noticed because I'd been dick whipped by Law and emotionally whipped by Ken? I was allowed to have a life regardless of my past decisions, right?

Nisha sniffed. "Sync, if something happened to you again, I'd never forgive myself. Hell, I wouldn't heal from that. Ever. You are my best friend. My sister. I only want the best for you. I want you to have love. A fulfilling relationship. But it needs to be the right one, not a toxic one. And I'm not saying that being with Law or Ken is toxic, I'm just saying slow down and test the waters so you can see whether they're right for you. That way you won't get into something where you mold yourself completely to them in a way that makes you forget who you are again and then you try to..."

She didn't need to finish her sentence. I knew what she was going to say but couldn't bring herself to say it. Tears flooded my eyes. She was right. That was exactly what had happened with Ken. I'd done everything he needed me to do. Been everything he needed me to be. Had even become a dog person and I hated dogs.

I wiped my eyes and fished inside my purse for a tissue, my vision quickly blurring.

"I hear you, Nisha, and I appreciate you being upfront with me. I can imagine how hard it was to go through that with me. I promise I'm good but now that you've brought this up, I will pull back because you're right, I can't go back down that road and I don't want to."

I felt her smile when I heard her relieved sigh through the speakers. "Thank you."

I couldn't help but smile back at the dashboard. "You're welcome."

The blaring beeping from the car caused my vision to snap toward the windshield. In front of me, Ken had stopped at a red light. I slammed on the brakes and closed my eyes, praying I'd stop in time.

That was the moment. The moment where I thought twice about Law. The moment where I thought twice about why I didn't suggest that Ken call a tow truck. The moment where I realized what my life had devolved into in only a week.

I never felt the impact. Didn't hear the eardrum shattering sound of the cars crashing into each other and becoming one. There was no taste of blood. I never heard the scream that propelled from my lungs.

What I felt were the tears rolling down my cheeks and wetting my shirt. What I heard was Ken banging on the driver's window, yelling my name and pleading for me to unlock the door. And what I finally saw wasn't something I would've wished on my worst enemy.

The replay of the moment I'd driven my car into a pole when I'd tried to take my life played vividly in front of my eyes. All of the feelings from that day, the pain I'd felt, hit me with a force that knocked me out. It was a time that my subconscious had blocked me from, ever since that day. Now, it was the only thing I could see.

Chapter 14

Complicated

1 Year Ago

I didn't like Aaron. He was simply a necessity. In the short month I'd known him and the few times we'd seen each other since, I'd already determined he wouldn't be someone I stayed with for the long-term. I was using him. Essentially, he was a distraction from the struggles I couldn't seem to overcome.

It hurt to be alone after all these years. Like, it really, really hurt. I wanted to call my parents to talk out the mess I'd made of my life, but they were gone. I needed my mom to listen to my problems just to tell me it'd be okay. To say that I'd make it through this troubling time. I needed her to say all that and then hang-up and call me back with my dad on the line, just like she always did. Then I needed them to tag team my problems until we hung up the phone with a game plan.

But they were gone. Had been gone for two whole years. Just like my brother. We were nine years apart, him being the oldest, and with the age gap, he'd been the best big brother I could have asked for. He never judged me for the choices I only confessed to him. He'd listen and then hug me until I released a super long deep breath, hold my hand as he spit out tough love, and rub my back until I recovered from pouting because I knew he was right.

And now, the last person I was officially family with was gone. The divorce papers had finally appeared at my door, delivered by a young man who asked my name, shoved the envelope in my hand, and then put his headphones in and disappeared. The most hurtful thing was Ken never called after the airport. He never texted. He just accepted that we were done as if he never loved me in the first place.

That's how I ended up here, parked on the suburban street across from Aaron's house. I needed somebody, anybody, to fill the void of my soon to be ex-husband. Someone to watch a movie and laugh with. I needed to be reminded that life could be normal once again.

I'd tried to find normal with Nisha but she struggled with the loss of my family almost as much as I did. We'd grown up as neighbors and I had a feeling that she'd been in a secret relationship with my brother. In time, she'd tell me and if she didn't want to say anything now, I was cool with that.

With Aaron, I didn't know what to expect. At first, I'd been intrigued by his lackadaisical attitude. The way he held easygoing conversations about everything from NASCAR racing to space exploration captured my interest for all of twenty-four hours. That quickly morphed into conversations where he constantly talked about himself and how and his frat used to run his college campus. He was stuck in the past but I guess, in a sense, so was I.

I activated the alarm on my Jetta and walked up his driveway. Right before my finger touched the doorbell, I paused. Something felt off but other than not knowing him well, I felt safe around him so I didn't know what could be throwing me off.

Aaron yanked open the door and stood there in slacks and

an old tee, as if he'd disposed of his dressier work shirt after arriving home. "I thought I heard you pull up."

"Yeah, just got here."

"Cool," he smiled. An odd smile. An unsexy one with smoker's teeth. "Come on in, Amber."

His home was as well taken care of inside as it was outside and I was immediately drawn to the picture on the mantel of two infant's newborn photos. One of a newborn in a diaper and headband with a bow. The other of a newborn in a diaper, resting his tiny chin on an even tinier fist. They were adorable and I'd always wanted kids. On the day that my family had been killed, Ken and I had finally decided to start trying but, yeah, guess it wasn't meant. If I were lucky enough to get married again hopefully we'd be blessed with a baby.

"You can sit on the sofa," he gestured to the middle of the room. "Want something to drink?"

"Water is fine." For now. In the confines of my small apartment, tequila was my go-to. During the day, at night, when I woke up, tequila was there for me, soothing my soul and numbing my feelings.

"I'll get you a bottle."

Before he rushed off, I asked, "Are these your babies?"

"Yeah. Twins."

He started to walk off again but I stopped him. "Aww, how cute. How old are they? What are their names?"

"I think they're about ten months. Might be eleven months though. Shit, I don't know."

"You did say they're your babies, didn't you?"

"Yeah, why?"

"You don't know how old they are?"

"Nah. Everything goes so fast in the first year, who can keep up? Shouldn't have to worry about months-only years. Their mom keeps up with that stuff so I don't need to."

I stood with my mouth open underneath the pictures and I prayed he was a better father than he made it seem.

When he returned, he handed me a frozen bottle of water. "Forgot to take it out the freezer. My bad. It'll be melted by the time you leave."

He licked his lips and all I felt was disgust. I wasn't ready to go there with another man. Or at least, I wasn't ready to go there with him. My recent one-night stand had been awful enough to prove I needed to keep my thighs glued.

I turned my attention to the TV and sat next to him. Close enough so he'd know I wasn't keeping my distance but far enough that he wouldn't get the impression that I wanted to stumble onto his lap.

We weren't even five minutes into a sports game I didn't want to watch before I heard a baby cry. I'd assumed the babies were with their mother at her place but the fact that they were upstairs while he was doing a piss poor job of romancing me grated on my nerves.

He didn't make a move to see about them so I asked, "Are you going to check on them?"

"Nah." Instead, he turned the volume higher on the TV.

"Well, I'd love to see them. Babies are so cute. I can go with you to see if they need something. Maybe their diaper is wet."

"Amber, relax. Georgia can handle them. She doesn't need my help. Trust me." On cue, the baby stopped crying.

I stared at him, my mouth slightly open and my eyes narrowed. There was someone upstairs with the babies? "Is Georgia their babysitter?"

He froze like he'd accidentally said too much, but then he sighed deeply and rolled his eyes. "She's their mom, Amber."

"Their mom," I repeated to myself, processing his words. There was not a sitter; there was a mother. To be exact, the baby's mother was upstairs. "Does she live here, too?"

"Yeah."

Jesus. This situation was quickly dissolving just like my life and processing it was already giving me a headache. With each word, my voice rose. "Are you and Georgia together? As in a relationship?"

After another long sigh his hand gestured and then fell back onto the arm of the sofa. "It's complicated."

Complicated. It was complicated. That seemed to be the answer for my life as of recent, but I could not take any more complications. Especially those induced by an outside party. The urge to leave pricked my skin and I buried my head in my hands. This man's babies and baby mama, or wife, or girlfriend, whoever the hell she was, was upstairs.

"I need more than it's complicated. Are you or are you not in a relationship with the woman upstairs?"

"Officially? Yes. Technically? No."

My stomach caved in as I leaned over, my elbows resting on my thighs. He turned to look at me but said nothing. "Aaron, stop skating over what I'm asking. Are you married? Is that your wife upstairs?"

"Yes. And yes."

"Oh my God!" I screamed.

He waved me off, unbothered by my discovery. "It's not like that, Amber. Chill out."

It was like that regardless of how he thought it was. I had to get out of there. Just as I stood to leave, Georgia descended the stairs.

"Who the fuck are you and why are you in my house?"

Chapter 15

The Count

You know the saying, shit hit the fan? Well, this was the shit and it had hit the fan. The shit had gone so high it was in the damn clouds and I was about to get shitted on. I stared at the woman I assumed was Georgia. She was gorgeous even though her distressed state read otherwise. Her dark, natural hair was pulled into a messy bun on the top of her head and her thin cotton robe was tied so that the sleeves hung uncoordinatedly over her shoulders. I could tell that at one time it had matched the slippers on her feet that were so worn she may as well have been barefoot.

Her tired, brown eyes narrowed as she scanned the room. Very slowly, reading the situation, reading me, reading Aaron, she descended the steps. I froze, fear of the unknown locking me in place. I was invited by Aaron but life really would've been so much better had I just declined it. I sighed and took a deep breath.

Georgia stopped moving at the bottom of the steps and crossed her arms. This was my rock bottom. It had to be. I'd gone from being someone's wife to being someone's mistress and it was hard to stomach.

Standing directly in front of my only escape, if I'd been able to actually get my feet to cooperate with my brain to run outside to my car, Georgia pointed at me. "I asked who the fuck you are and I know you heard me the first time."

"I, umm, my name..."

In the calmest of voices, she stated, "No, I don't need to know your goddamn name. Who are you to my husband and why the hell are you in my house?"

There was no easy way to explain unless Aaron, who was irritatingly quiet, stepped in. And I had an inkling or two that he would do no such thing, which left me with two options. I could plead for forgiveness and hope she sent me on my way, or I could claw my way out. The thought of having to pick one made my blood turn cold.

As I watched her turn the locks on the door my hands turned clammy and a cold sweat broke out across my neck. She crossed her arms and leaned against it. I had to give her an answer and I just prayed it was the right one.

"Well Aaron and I were chatting and..." No, that wouldn't work. It was at that moment that I knew it really didn't matter what I said. Nothing was going to make her feel better and whatever I said would probably make things worse. I settled on, "I'm not supposed to be here..."

"You damn right you aren't."

"But umm, so here's the thing. Aaron invited me over tonight. I thought he was single and didn't know he was married until right before you came downstairs and when I found out I was like, "This ain't what I signed up for," so I was getting ready to leave. I certainly didn't even know you were here so I'll just see myself out."

I waited. And waited. And waited. But she didn't move from in front of that damn door. The only indication that she'd heard me was her death stare that held me in place. "You'll stay right there until I get to the bottom of this."

How many times could I curse my life today? The Count from Sesame Street started counting in my head, mocking me. One fucked life, ah ah. Two fucked lives, ah ah. I swallowed.

Georgia turned her attention to Aaron. "Is this your girl? Your boo? Your mistress?"

I internally pleaded for him to answer her question the right way. Whether that meant he told her I was no one or that I had delivered some food, I just hoped he didn't screw this up for the both of us. I chanced a glance at him, praying for him to say the best thing.

"Why do you care, Georgia?"

Three fucked lives, ah ah. Of all the things he could've said, that was what he chose? I cringed, squeezing my eyes shut when Georgia's head slowly tilted to the side and she raised an eyebrow.

"Are you fucking kidding me right now?" Georgia yelled.

"Are you fucking kidding me, Georgia?" Aaron retorted. "Don't act like you're some kind of innocent bystander."

"You have another woman in my house and you're trying to pin that on me?" She looked at me and I averted my eyes, not wanting to make eye contact. "*This* is the kind of man that you're attracted to?"

No, and if I were honest with myself, I didn't even know what I was attracted to anymore, but I knew he wasn't it. I'd known that before I trucked it to his house to seek out his attention. It was desperation at its worst. How could I explain to her that I wasn't, in the least bit, interested in her husband? That I wasn't trying to break up a home. That I was here because I'd been trying to fill a void after I'd broken up my own happy home.

"At this point I'd just like to go home and pretend none of this ever happened. I don't want to cause any more harm."

"How often do you see my husband?"

I tried not to sigh. "This is my first time meeting him."

"So, that's what you do then? Go to a man's house on the first date? You're either a hoe or you're lying to me. Which is it?"

I gasped, "Neither."

"Were you two supposed to go somewhere then? On a date?"

"Not to my knowledge." I looked at Aaron but he'd sat back down on the sofa and seemed uninterested in our conversation. Perfect.

"Uh uh," Georgia snapped her fingers to get my attention. "I'm asking you questions. Don't look to him for answers."

As an innocent bystander, I became angry that her energy was directed at me. I was just as mad as her. Aaron had put both of us in a terrible situation. "I promise, I didn't know he was married. He never said he was. And he never said he had kids."

"Convenient for you, huh? The victim."

"I wouldn't say so considering this," I motioned around the room.

She slowly nodded and then her eyes narrowed to a slit. "Aaron! Look at me! Are you even going to try and explain what the hell is going on or are you going to sit on your ass like you always do?"

He shrugged. "What don't you understand? This is my girl, Amber."

My eyes bulged out and I took another step away from him, vigorously shaking my head. "No, don't tell those lies. I am not your girl. We barely know each other."

Georgia sucked her teeth and nodded once before walking towards us. Stalking closer with every step. I didn't want to fight, especially over Aaron. I was a lover. I'd never fought one person or lifted my hands in an attempt to, but if she came at me, I would swing my way out if I had to.

Aaron, seeing her walking toward us, stood up and came closer to me. If this was his way of protecting me I was here for it. Maybe he would finally stop this madness and I could get out of here. I could escape. She reared up to smack one of us and I braced for impact.

The Count started up again. Four fucked lives, ah ah.

But with an act of God, my ass was saved. Behind us was the most beautiful sound. Sliding down the stairs on their belly, a little baby giggled with each bounce down.

Georgia looked at her baby, then at her outstretched arm, and then at Aaron and me. Tears sprang up in her eyes before her mouth dropped open. She covered her mouth with both hands. "What am I doing? I can't-I can't do this anymore."

Aaron, ignoring us, walked to the stairs and picked up the baby. "My little escape artist has done it again. Haven't you sweetheart?"

This distraction should have been my cue to bounce but my heart was splitting by the second. No woman deserved this type of pain and I hated that I had, unbeknownst, contributed to breaking another woman's heart. As she cried, I started to cry with her. "I'm sorry. I didn't know."

"Go to hell," she lashed out at me and I just nodded. That's all I could do. If she needed to be mad at me, that was fine. I could take it. She ran upstairs and I realized that was my cue. My moment to escape. I grabbed my purse but it felt lighter. I shook it and the familiar jingle of my keys didn't ring out.

Five fucked lives, ah ah.

God had to be playing some kind of joke on me because surely, this couldn't be life right now. At this point I was ready to drop onto the floor with a white surrender flag. I could not seriously be stranded in the home where a wife had just caught her husband cheating with me. Nisha would have a field day with this if I had to call her to pick me up.

But I wasn't there yet. I had to keep going. Had to think. Where could I have left or dropped my keys? I tapped my forehead repeatedly hoping to somehow, jog my memory. I'd only walked from the door to the sofa and I'd brought them inside with me so they had to be somewhere. I scanned the end table but they weren't there. Nor were they underneath. I looked back to the spot on the sofa where I'd sat before all hell broke loose but they weren't there either. I slipped my hands between the cushions, all of them, flipping each one up but my keys were nowhere to be found.

"Shit." I put the cushions back in their places.

Aaron turned to me. "What are you looking for?"

"My keys!"

"You say that like I knew already."

"Why else would I still be here?"

He shrugged and stared at me as if I didn't understand simple English. "Because you were staying."

"Staying?" I shrieked, my voice reaching a pitch I'd never heard before. "No, you idiot. Why would I stay? You lied to me. You lied to your wife. You put me in an awkward situation where in a span of like, thirty minutes, I was confronted, degraded, and humiliated! No woman in her right mind would stay here with you."

Aaron raised his eyebrows and sighed. "Your loss." He went back to bouncing his baby until his jaw squared.

I turned around to see what had caught his attention. Georgia was coming down the stairs with her other baby and bags of what I assumed were clothing and supplies. She'd changed into an oversized tee and jeans that were a size too small.

Aaron and I watched. As a mother who'd done it hundreds of times already, she opened the stroller sitting by the door with one arm, buckled the baby in, placed the diaper bag into the bottom storage of the stroller, and then dropped the rest of her bags on the floor. She then walked over to Aaron and demanded, "Give me my baby."

Chapter 16

Broken

"YOU DON'T CARE ANYTHING ABOUT ME OR OUR BABIES SO GIVE her to me." Georgia stood, her nose flared, and her gaze locked on Aaron. She was not playing games and the only thing I feared was how far she'd go to get the baby out of Aaron's hands if he refused to hand her over.

"*Your* babies? They're *our* babies. Unless you have something to tell me."

Oh no he didn't. Or, oh no she didn't? Shit. I was all the way in this soap opera mess. Wrapping one arm around my waist and lifting my other hand to my mouth, I began to bite my nails. I wasn't even a nail biter but I didn't know what else to do. The last place anyone ever wanted to be was stuck between was some marital drama and I happened to be less than a foot away.

A quick laugh escaped from Georgia. "Ha! If only dreams came true. Unfortunately, Aaron, you are the father. Not only are you stuck being their parent for the rest of your life but I'm attached to your low life ass for the rest of mine. Now hand over my baby."

"You take one and I'll take the other."

Everyone in the room stopped moving. This man had the biggest balls. Splitting up twins had to be the most devastating thing a parent could ever suggest.

"The hell I will!" Georgia yelled. "The twins stay together and they stay with me-the parent who takes care of them all day and night while you only take care of yourself."

"Bullshit. I take care of my kids."

"What's the last thing you did for them, Aaron?" When it took a second too long for him to answer, Georgia raised her eyebrows. "Can't think of anything can you?"

"At least I don't leave them in an unsafe environment. How did baby girl get out of her crib again? What would've happened if I weren't down here?"

"You do one thing right and wanna act like you a goddamn king." Georgia reached out and looped her hands under the baby's arms to pick her up but Aaron pulled away, still holding the baby.

My stomach dropped as I watched them both try to get the upper hand without harming their little girl. When she started to cry, I yelled, "Stop!" and stepped between them, attempting to pull them apart. But Georgia turned on me and pushed me backwards so hard that I stumbled onto the couch, rolling my ankle in the process. I reached for my foot and winced.

Georgia followed me over with menace in her eyes. "If you ever touch me again, I will do more than push your ass down. Don't fuck with me." She turned back to Aaron, "Now you, give me my baby." When he still held on tight, she said it again, "Give her to me! You don't want kids. All you want is to be a bum ass nigga."

A snarl appeared on his face before he handed over their baby. "Take her. You'll be back."

Georgia bounced the baby and soothed her before strapping her into the stroller. "Wishful thinking," she hissed.

"You ain't got a job. You don't have any money. You ain't got nowhere to go. So yeah, you'll be back. You think I'm worthless but you need to take a good look in the mirror. What do you do, Georgia? You don't cook. You don't clean. All you care about are these kids. What about me?"

"What about you nigga? Why would anyone care about you? What do you do other than play video games all day? You're not even good for sex. The last time I came close to coming was when I popped the kids out my pussy. Good luck finding another bitch that fakes it as good as me."

Aaron waved her off. "Hoes always wanna talk about a nigga dick after the fact knowing good damn well they was screaming that nigga name the night before. Like I said, you'll be back. Ain't nobody gonna take care of a broken ass woman and her fucking babies."

Georgia's mouth quivered as she tried, unsuccessfully, to not cry. I hoped that she believed she wasn't broken and I prayed she had somewhere to go. With her hand on the door handle, she said, "I'll live in a women's shelter before I come back to a house with no love."

When she opened the door, a woman stood on the other side with her hand up, ready to knock. Georgia simply looked at her and said, "I can't do this anymore." And I felt that, more than I probably should have. Keys or no keys, as soon as Georgia left, I was hobbling my ass right out after her.

I watched as her friend jumped into action, taking bags off Georgia's arms and then a fine ass man walked in and picked up more of Georgia's things. If I didn't feel bad already, the look of disgust that he gave Aaron and me confirmed that I was the scum everyone thought I was.

Once he stepped out, Aaron walked across the room and locked the door, eventually coming to sit back down next to me. I couldn't help but to roll my eyes. It was then that I caught sight of my water bottle on the mantel and it dawned on me that I'd stopped there to look at the pictures of their babies.

And thank God, my keys were right next to it. I had put them down when Aaron handed me the bottle of water. I got up to grab them but fell back down when I put pressure on my ankle. "Shit!" I lifted my ankle to rub it and realized it had swelled.

When Georgia knocked on the door and screamed for Aaron to open it, he turned the TV volume higher. Knowing that he would continue to disregard her, I called on all of my energy and pain management to get up from the sofa. If he wasn't going to open the door, I would. I was leaving anyway.

But I didn't make it in time because the door panel flew off with a loud bang and Georgia walked in with a gun.

Fifty fucked lives, ah ah.

I didn't feel an ounce of pain as I held my hands in the air and hobbled my way over to a chair. Sitting down, I refused to make eye contact with anyone in that room. Everything that happened after that was a blur but before Georgia left, she looked behind her one last time and said, "Aaron, in case you haven't figured this out, I want a divorce."

AFTER ALL WAS SAID AND EVERYTHING WAS DONE, I SAT IN MY driveway and cried. And cried some more. Not having the strength to get out of my car after I'd driven home, I'd stayed inside like I was a hostage. I'd made a mess of my life. A whole, complete mess.

I missed Ken like crazy. I missed coming home after work and watching TV. I even missed having to feed Ken's dumb dog when he went out of town. They were the simplest of things but I needed simple to come back.

Life was ridiculously hard since our split and the worst part of all of this was realizing that I hadn't asked for a divorce because I'd been unhappy. I'd purposely pushed Ken away. It was like, if I couldn't have my mom, dad, or brother, then I didn't deserve Ken.

It was my fault that my family had died. I had called them when they were on their way to my house for a Memorial Day cookout. I had requested they pick up a bottle of BBQ sauce.

Instead of calling Nisha to walk to the store that was next door to her place, I'd called my dad. Instead of asking Ken to step away from the grill, I'd called my dad. Instead of pushing pause on the series I was binging, I called my dad.

I didn't deserve happiness and happiness, or at least contentment, was what I felt when with Ken. A flood of tears and snot ran down my face and I screamed until my throat hurt. "God, why? Why?" My body shook as I pounded the windows, the steering wheel, the center console-anything I could touch with my hands.

Guilt threatened to close my throat as the memories broke me. Again. They'd all died because I'd forgotten to pick up fucking BBQ sauce.

"Hello."

"Daddy," I sang into the phone when he answered through his car's speakerphone.

"Hey, Am," he returned.

Jumping in, my mom said, "We're on the way. The gips…"

My brother laughed in the background. "Mom, for the last time, it's G-P-S, not gips. You have to pronounce every letter."

I shook my head; my mother was stubborn and would always say it that way regardless of how many times we corrected her. "I don't know why you keep trying to get her to say it right."

"Anyway," she ignored us like always, "we'll be there in twenty minutes. We just left your brother's place."

"Yeah," my brother yelled from far away. I assumed he was in the back seat. "Remind me to never ride with these crazy two again."

"Noted," I laughed. "Ken just took the hot dogs off the grill so I'll tell him to put your steaks on so they're nice and fresh when you get here. And can y'all stop and get BBQ sauce? I forgot to get it yesterday when I picked up everything."

"What kind do you want?" my dad asked.
"I know what kind she likes," my mom said.
"Thank you, Mommy. See you soon. Love you."
A chorus of I love yous responded.

That was the last time I heard their voices. After they left the store, they'd gotten a flat tire while on the highway. Always one to do things according to the book instead of changing it with my brother, my dad lit flares and waited for roadside assistance. But roadside assistance took longer than expected because of the holiday. A simple text had told me that much and the police had told me the rest.

Two drivers, who'd had a bit to drink, were also on their way to a friend's house for a cookout. Wanting to have a little fun, they decided to race each other. They only had five more minutes until they reached their destination. Five minutes. On the last curve of their journey, everyone's lives changed. The older of the two who'd been winning, lost control. His car jumped the median, spun out, and crashed into my family. When they collided, his vehicle was moving at over a hundred miles an hour. He, and my family, were killed on impact.

As some form of cruelty, the only thing salvageable from the car was one thing. I'd had to cremate my family but on the side of the road, still in the grocery tote, was the bottle of BBQ sauce.

Chapter 17

Back to the Future

My phone wouldn't stop ringing and as hard as I tried, I couldn't get my hand to cooperate in order to pick up the damn thing and silence it. My fingertips sloppily slid down my swaying head and as soon as I touched the cold screen, I was out cold again.

When I awoke, my eyelids were even heavier. With no awareness of how long I'd been passed out, or where I was, I managed to remember why I was still in my car after leaving Aaron's. Sitting there, windows down, music low, mind in a haze, it was time. I was going Home and I felt an enormous amount of peace over my decision. It wasn't something I took lightly. No, this decision was a long time coming. I just wasn't happy anymore. I had tried to find happiness after my family died but it just did not exist. And nothing that anyone did or said, changed that. Not my therapist. Not Ken. And not Nisha.

Everything in my life, including me, was fucked up and I was tired of trying to fix it. With each progressive move, another stream of bad news or awful luck, such as Aaron, appeared and backhanded the shit outta me. Putting in enormous effort to only make one small step forward was exhausting and I was tired of hoping tomorrow would be a better day. It was time to reunite with my family.

I smiled at the thought, hoping my mommy would be happy to see me. And my dad and brother too. And of course, my Creator. Sure, I'd be arriving Home earlier than they expected, but as long as they still believed that everything happened as it was supposed to, I'd be right on time.

I took a deep breath and harshly blew it out. I had to get this over with before I passed out again. The time on my dashboard read two thousand and twenty-two. Two thousand? I blinked a few times, wincing as I tried to get my vision to cooperate. "Jesus Christ," I mumbled, unable to get my eyes to focus.

My phone started ringing again. Nisha. I'd sent her an emotional goodbye that I expected her to read in the morning but she had to have seen it already. She never called in the middle of the night unless it was an emergency and for her, stopping me from completing my mission was an emergency. Once my phone chirped with the missed call notification I turned it off. I didn't need her using my location to track my whereabouts. I was going through with this. I only needed to figure out how to turn my car on.

I peeked at the lit dashboard. Okay, so my car was already on. Sighing, I took one last look at the trees, wondering if they existed in Heaven. If not, I sure was going to miss them. But one thing I wouldn't miss was the daily emotional and physical pain that came along with just being alive. Having to fight through stress and anger, and sadness and negativity was for the birds. If it wasn't one thing it was surely another and I found it hard to believe that before leaving Heaven, my spirit signed up and agreed to go through this bullshit.

Right as I got ready to try and put my car into drive, a bright light shined through my open window into my face. I raised my forearm to block the brightness. Squinting, I noticed a uniformed officer standing outside, beaming his flashlight into my car.

"Everything alright in here, Ma'am?"

Everything would be perfect as soon as he left. I just had to keep it together long enough to convince him to go. My dry tongue scraped my lips and I blinked a few times before I managed a hoarse, "Fine."

"Ma'am, have you been drinking tonight?" His eyes narrowed on the spilled bottle of pills in my passenger seat. "Are you under the influence of any narcotics?"

Wouldn't he like to know. I laughed at my joke as I looked over the few pills left. I hadn't a clue on how many I'd taken but couldn't have been that many. There were still five...or ten-I sighed, unable to count the pills.

"Step out of the car for me."

"I-I-I." Come on, you can do it. You can finish a sentence. "I-I." Fuck. I gave up on talking since nothing coherent was coming out. Instead, I put my pointer finger in the air to tell him to hold on and I went to shift from park. "Bye."

"No, do not put the car in drive!" He quickly stashed his flashlight and pulled on the door handle. "Unlock the doors, Ma'am."

"I-I have to go now. Something important to be. I mean do."

He began yelling, "Ma'am, do not put the car in drive! Get out of the car!" He used his radio to call for assistance and then yanked on the handle again, fumbling inside the car to find the button to unlock the doors.

As best I could, I pushed his hands back outside but he was persistent. Smiling, I swatted his hand and commanded him to stop. "Bad boy."

"No, *you* stop," he countered, still trying to unlock my doors with an unbelievable strength. Each time I pushed him away his hands returned like they were never removed.

"*No*, you stop."

His hands gripped the door and through tight lips, he looked at me, took a second to get his breath, and firmly said, "I need you to get out of your car."

Not a chance in hell. Which is where we were currently. With a contented smile, I gazed up at him. "See you on the other side."

I clumsily fumbled with the gearshift until I remembered that to put it in drive, I first had to put my foot on the brake. Seeing what I was about to do, the officer poked his head through the window and located the unlock button. He yanked open the door but it was too late.

With the car in the right gear, my heavy foot found the gas pedal. I floored it, my car speeding away with the officer running behind me, yelling for me to stop. Not happening, Buddy. Not happening.

I glanced out the window to take my last look at those big, beautiful trees whizzing past. Yeah, I was going to miss them. Back in front of me, my destiny beckoned. My fingers slipped several times before I finally found the push button to unbuckle my seatbelt. I slipped it from around me and took my hands off the wheel. One arm outside the window, the other stretched to the passenger side holding the peace sign up, I prayed that when this was over, I'd wake up on the other side.

PRESENT DAY

Noise. There was so much noise. Ken banged on the window, trying to get my attention. "Amber! Unlock the doors. Amber!"

Then, there was Nisha yelling through the car's speakers, repeatedly calling my name. "Sync! Answer me, what's going on? Did you get in an accident? Please, God, let her be okay. Sync!" she cried.

My chest rose rapidly as I took in my surroundings. My whole body shook as I looked in front of me to assess the damage, but there wasn't any. I'd stopped in time. I stopped in time and didn't hit Ken. The banging on the window and the screaming through the speakers continued as I tried to calm an impending panic attack.

I called on lessons learned in therapy. Putting one hand over my heart and the other over my navel, I said, "I am safe. I am unharmed. The sky is blue. My eyes are brown. The steering wheel is beige. I hear beeping. Birds are chirping. Cars are honking." I continued repeating things I knew to be true, such as my address and age to confirm to my unconscious that I was truly, not under duress. By the time I'd finished, my breathing was almost back to normal.

"Sync? Are you talking to me? What are you saying? I don't understand." Nisha's higher than normal voice proved how panicked she was.

"I'm okay, Nisha." My voice still quivered but I was okay.

"You're okay? You're sure, Sync? All I heard was beeping and then you were screaming..."

"I was screaming?"

"Yes!" She spoke fast. "And then I didn't hear anything and I didn't know if you were okay or what had happened. What happened? Did you get in an accident?"

"No. No accident. Close call though. Thank God for safety features." I scrubbed my hand down my face and wiped my tears. "I can't believe that just happened. Ken would've killed me if I put a scratch in his car."

I turned toward him and his reddened face relaxed as he took in my appearance. Directing my attention back to Nisha, I said, "I'll explain later. Call you soon." I then ended the call and unlocked the doors.

Ken pulled open the door and wrapped me in his arms.

"God, Amber, what's wrong? You're crying. Are you hurt?" He held me at arm's length to check for visible injuries. Seeing none, he pulled me back into his embrace.

"I remembered. I remembered everything." I laid on his chest in a trance from the unlocked memories. Whether from the drugs or PTSD, I'd completely forgotten everything about that night. I hadn't even remembered the situation with Aaron. Trauma was a bitch whose only goal in life was to fuck me raw.

"You remembered what?" Ken pulled his body far enough away to stare into my eyes.

My fingers gripped the sides of his shirt, trying to ground myself to something. The confusion in his eyes reminded me that when we'd parted, and subsequently divorced, we hadn't talked. He had no idea of the dark tunnel I'd crawled through to put my life back together. As far as he knew, I hadn't been depressed. I hadn't attempted suicide. I hadn't needed to recover from anything except the loss of our marriage. And because of that, Sync didn't exist, only Amber.

I gently pulled out of his embrace to breathe in this moment, to finally realize and embrace the harmony after the storm. Yes, I'd been through the trenches, fought my way back to reality, and continued to dig out of quicksand, but without all of that, I wouldn't be Sync, the woman who survived losing it all. Sure, a piece of my heart was still empty, and would most likely always be, but without my downfall, I wouldn't be who I am today.

"Amber?"

"I just, umm, I remembered how precious life is." I wasn't ready to expose my soul or explain that time of my life to Ken, nor did I know if I'd ever be ready.

He pulled me back in tight. "You're right. I'm so happy you're okay."

And so was I. To some, peace, joy, and happiness looked

like being on a beach, drink in hand. For me, peace looked like living my life on my terms and allowing myself the freedom to be sad about the loss I'd endured. Joy meant allowing myself to feel unexpected butterflies after meeting a guy at the library. Best of all, happiness came from staying in sync.

Chapter 18

With Love

I SAT ON MY SOFA STARING OUT THE WINDOW, WATCHING THE snow lightly drift past. In the background, the narrator of the show I was trying to watch spoke of a neighbor turned deadly. I'd rewound the show four times already and still hadn't a clue what had happened. My thoughts were less on the programming and more on everything that went down in my life last month. I'd had a time, I'd had a time.

The emotional turbulence I'd experienced during that week and a half had equaled the total despair I'd felt over the last few years. I felt lighter after finally being able to put my feelings in place but it'd taken some time to get there.

So much had gone down in such a short period of time that afterwards, I'd cut everyone off. Ken, Nisha, Law-I'd blocked them all while I got back in sync. My life was of utmost importance and if I didn't know where I was headed then I couldn't see who deserved to be in my future.

Fortunately, it hadn't taken too much time to bring Nisha back in. She was my ride or die. My soulmate who always had my best interests at heart. My sounding board that kept me sane with injected spurts of calculated audacity. There was no way I could have moved forward without her. We shared similar goals and the same wrenching heart break of lost loved ones.

And Ken. My sweet Ken. We'd finally talked. We'd argued. Cried. We'd almost kissed. At the end, he understood that I'd lost myself while we were married and that it wasn't anything he'd done or didn't do to cause that. I still loved and appreciated him and because of that I would always hold space for him in my heart. Eventually, that love would fade but I knew I'd always care deeply for him. That care had been tested one day when I'd decided to pop up on him to drop off a bag of chips. It was a thoughtful gesture but it was one that no longer fit into our lives for the place that our relationship had evolved to.

I'd noticed an unknown car in his driveway and right as I closed my car door, the woman Ken had been with at the rink walked out the front door. I'd seen the goofy smile on Ken's face enough times to know the woman hadn't just stopped by to say hi.

Of course I knew he would move on, had expected it, but to see him enjoy another woman in the same way he had enjoyed me had been the reality check I needed. I wanted him to be happy, to enjoy life however he saw fit, with whomever he saw fit to do it with, especially since I hadn't decided what role I wanted to play in his life. To allow that to happen I had to completely let him go. He didn't need me muddling his thoughts. Maybe we'd find our way back to each other, but for now, our time had come to an end.

Then, there was Law. I never figured out what it was about him that attracted me to the point where I bypassed my morals but with there always being something about him, he had to go so I could continue my healing journey. For that reason, I'd invited him over to officially return his coat. Any minute now, he would arrive and I'd be able to close another door to my past. We hadn't seen or talked since my near accident and with his handsome face splayed on my doorbell camera my body immediately conjured up wild memories.

He leaned closer to the camera with a wild smile. "Open up Shawty I got good news."

I couldn't help but smile into my phone. He was so damn sexy it didn't make sense and I hoped I'd remain strong enough to break it off with him despite his good news. But as soon as I opened my door, he picked me up, shutting the door with his foot. When my back hit the wall, I gasped.

My God, Jesus be a fence between me and Law's dick.

His hardened brown eyes stared into mine right before he kissed me and it was delicious. "Damn I missed you. Why you make me wait so long to see you?"

It was *just like old times*. If there was a such thing as a sexual soulmate, he had to be mine. It sounds wild; we'd only slept together twice. And maybe it was from his seemingly massive amount of experience and the lack of mine, but damn if his soft lips didn't feel like pillows on my neck as they traveled down the side. He alternated between firm sucks to circular motions with his tongue. My legs wrapped around him, I knew I had to stop this before I forgot why I'd called him over. But then he squeezed my ass and ground into me.

"Law," I gasped when he pressed his erection into my core.

"Shawty you know you can't be saying my name like that. We won't make it to the bed. I'll have your legs spread right here on this floor." My pussy leaked with thoughts of him pounding into me on top of my area rug.

I gently pushed away, prompting him to playfully nip my shoulder before placing me on the floor. "You, uh, you said you had good news for me?"

"Right," he snapped his fingers. "My girl broke up with me."

"Oh. Okay."

He took a short step back, studying me. "Okay? That's all you got to say?"

I shrugged. "What did you want me to say?"

"Shit, I don't know. Something other than that. Thought you'd be happy or something. I mean you ghosted me so I thought you was struggling with me being with my girl, even though I already told you that shit was complicated."

I was happy they were no longer together but that wouldn't alter how I wanted to move on. "You happy she broke up with you?"

Little lines appeared on his forehead as he thought about my question. "I mean, she was cool but our relationship was done a long time ago."

"Why didn't you ever break up with her?"

"Wanted it to be her decision."

I crossed my arms over my chest. "So what was the straw that broke the camel's back?"

"Hell if I know," he rubbed his chin. "You really ain't got nothin' to say about me being single?"

"No," I released an awkward chuckle. "I actually called you over to return your coat."

"Damn, for real?"

"Yeah."

"It don't matter that I'm single huh?"

I shook my head, confirming my answer within myself and for him. "No."

"You cutthroat." A smile spread across his face making me return it. "I'm going to miss your smile. You remember when you was at my spot and you wanted to fuck one more time?"

I swallowed, knowing where he was headed. He bit his bottom lip and hooked his finger in the waistband of my leggings, dragging me toward him. He spoke low, making sure we were clear. "I'ma let you go but not before diving in this pussy. One. Last. Time."

"Okay," I breathed out. There wasn't anything wrong with a one last time situation. Right? Goosebumps popped up all over my skin in anticipation of what it would be like. Would he take me fast? Would we do all the things or just some?

He lifted my arms above my head and held my wrists together. "If you was any other girl I woulda just walked out the door but you different. I swear you put some spell on me cuz my dick ain't been the same since I met you. It's gon' be hard to let you go."

It'd be hard to let him go too but he was never mine anyway. I would do well to remember that. He walked me backwards to my couch, tonguing me down the whole way, and swiftly rid me of my leggings and my soaked panties.

"I wanna take it slow since this our last time and all but fuck." He pushed my legs into the air and slapped my ass cheek. I moaned in delight. His eyebrow rose right before he pushed inside me and bottomed out in one swift stroke. I screamed out, happy we were here and could be as loud and wild as we wanted. Even if it was the last time.

"Don't move," he said through tight lips. Easy for him to say. He wasn't the one nearing an instant orgasm. With one arm wrapped around my calves, he used the other to lift my shirt and undo the front clasp of my bra. My breasts freely spilled into his waiting hand. Held hostage, I internally begged him to move just an inch. I was going to come so fast. I squeezed around him, causing him to grunt in response.

"I guess you waited long enough." He took his time thrusting in and out, his breath shooting out with each push into me. "You got the best pussy I ever had. Goddamn Sync."

Our bodies clapped against each other and with each stroke I sunk deeper into the sofa.

"Ahh shit," he said when my legs started shaking. "You 'bout to come already?"

"Yes," I rasped.

"You know what to do then. Or else I ain't gonna let you."

"Ooo Law," I whined.

"Hell yeah. That's right. You gonna make me come too Shawty." Faster and faster he pushed into me, building up the tension below my waist. He lifted my hips and drove into me like a madman, cussing the entire time. I came as hard as I thought I would, temporarily losing my vision when my eyes clamped shut.

Law was right behind me as he yelled out, "Say my name again."

My pussy clamped down once more, milking him for all he had. "Law!"

"Fuuuck!" He released into the condom and froze over top of me, one drop of sweat falling onto my chest. His body propped over mine, he waited to catch his breath before kissing me again, slow and easy.

"I'll be right back." Pants around his ankles, he waddled off to the bathroom and I pulled my panties and leggings back on. A few minutes later he walked back into the room, phone in hand. "Aye, I gotta make a run. I'll hit you up later."

He bent down to kiss my forehead and said bye but there couldn't be a later. There wouldn't be a later. This was our goodbye. I got up from the sofa and walked to the chair. "Wait a minute. Here, take your coat."

His eyes traveled from my face to the coat in my outstretched arm. "You sure, Shawty?"

I nodded. "Yeah. I had fun with you though."

"A'ight, Cutthroat," he joked. He walked back over and laid a gentle kiss on my lips and then another on my forehead, his lips lingering in a last goodbye. "You know how to reach me if you change your mind."

"I do." With that, Law left. I sat in the emptiness of my home, happy to have stood firm in my decision. I did want a relationship but I wanted one that felt right. I wanted someone who would court me, respect me, and someone who'd accept my past, present, and future. They would have to love me as

Sync Amber Patterson. I didn't know who that would be or when it would happen, but I was content with waiting my turn.

I dropped onto my sofa and stared at my cold cup of tea until my phone beeped with a text notification. My mouth dropped open when I saw the name.

> Hey Sync. You never responded to my text but I can't forget how you looked in that red coat. Just beautiful. So I'm giving it one last shot. If you're free I'd love to meet you at the library and go for ice cream after. Today or tomorrow?

Isaiah. I guess it was true what they said. When you ridded yourself of the wrong things it gave the right things a chance to find you.

I responded,

> Hello Stranger. I'd like that. How about next week though?

He sent a gif of a man excitedly pumping his fist in the air, which made me laugh.

I know what you're thinking; I should slow down.

You might be right, but we'll see.

With Love, Sync Amber Patterson.

About the Author

Chichima Cherry is an award-winning author who is always down to tell a story, eat a sweet and spicy pickle, or chew gum (not necessarily in that order.) She resides in Indianapolis with her husband, kiddos, and Hawke Man the dog. In addition to writing fiction, she writes children's books under her late mom's name, Karen Mae.

In her free time she wifes, mothers her 3 wild childs, reads, bakes, works on puzzles, and runs.

instagram.com/chichimacherry

tiktok.com/@corieverafter

bookbub.com/profile/chichima-cherry

goodreads.com/chichimacherry

amazon.com/author/chichimacherry

corieverafter.substack.com

About Write and Vibe

We are an independent publishing company that believes writers should only have to worry about writing. Meaning, you write your book, we'll do the rest.

To learn more about us, our authors, and their books, please visit us at

Writeandvibe.com | Fb & IG @writeandvibe

www.ingramcontent.com/pod-product-compliance
Lightning Source LLC
Chambersburg PA
CBHW071946190726
48293CB00004B/1373